"What possessed you to tell such lies?"

When Sarah didn't answer, Radolf went on to ask, "Because I was home?"

"Well, yes, I suppose so."

"I see. In future, you will take your day off when I am here so there'll be no need for us to meet." Radolf glanced at her. "Will that suit you?"

Sarah wanted to agree with dignity but instead, she felt her throat close over tears that were going to burst into a flood at any moment.

Everything had gone wrong; he was coldhearted and mean and arrogant and she loved him to distraction....

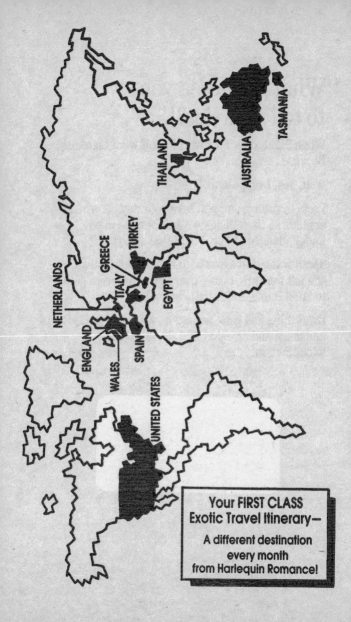

NETHERLANDS
ENGLAND
WALES
GREECE
ITALY
SPAIN
TURKEY
EGYPT
THAILAND
AUSTRALIA
TASMANIA
UNITED STATES

Your FIRST CLASS
Exotic Travel Itinerary—

A different destination
every month
from Harlequin Romance!

ROSES HAVE THORNS
Betty Neels

Harlequin Books

TORONTO • NEW YORK • LONDON
AMSTERDAM • PARIS • SYDNEY • HAMBURG
STOCKHOLM • ATHENS • TOKYO • MILAN

Original hardcover edition published in 1990
by Mills & Boon Limited

ISBN 0-373-03149-1

Harlequin Romance first edition September 1991

ROSES HAVE THORNS

CHAPTER ONE

SARAH sat behind her desk and watched the first of the patients for Professor Nauta's clinic come in through the swing-doors. Led, as usual, by old Colonel Watkins, recovering for the third time from a stroke and eighty if he was a day. The Professor's clinic started at half-past eight and it had become Sarah's responsibility, although she wasn't sure how it had happened, to come on duty early in order to check his patients; the other two receptionists, married ladies with homes, husbands and children to cope with, were adamant about leaving exactly on time and not a minute later, just as they arrived exactly when they should and not a moment sooner. So that Professor Nauta's clinic, held weekly at eight-thirty, invariably fell to the lot of Sarah, who, being single, living alone and therefore from their point of view without cares, was the obvious one of the trio to come early or stay late.

The Colonel was followed by Mrs Peach, who had been coming for years, and hard on her heels came a pair of teenagers, giving their names with a good deal of giggling, and after them a steady stream of people, most of whom Sarah knew by sight if not by name. She bade each one of them good morning, made sure that the new patients knew what was wanted of them, and ticked off her neat list. There were five minutes to go before the half-hour when the last patient arrived, and exactly on the half-hour the Professor came through the swing-doors, letting in a great deal of chilly March air. Sarah took a quick look at him and decided that he seemed no more impatient and ill-tempered than usual. He was a very big man, tall and broad-shouldered and good-looking, with fair hair already grey at the temples, a high-bridged nose and a thin mouth. His eyes were pale blue which turned to steel when he was annoyed—which was quite often, although it was conceded by those who worked for him at St Cyprian's that he was invariably kindness itself to his patients, however tiresome they were.

He went past Sarah's desk with a snappy, 'Good morning, Miss Fletcher,' and a glance so brief that he couldn't have noticed if she had been wearing a blonde wig and spectacles. She would have been very surprised to know that he had taken in her appearance down to the last button as he'd gone past her. Small, a little too thin, pleasant-faced without being pretty, beautiful pansy eyes, a thin, delicate nose, a wide mouth and a crown of hair which took her some considerable time to put up each morning. He had noted her sparkling white blouse, too, and the fact that she wore nothing which jangled, only a sensible wristwatch. A sensible young woman, he reflected briefly, as neat as a new pin and not given to chat. Not all that young—late twenties, perhaps, although she had the freshness of a young girl. He reached his consulting-room, greeting the nurse waiting for him, and sat down at his desk, dismissing Miss Fletcher from his mind without effort, listening to Colonel Watkins' tetchy old voice complaining about the treatment he was having at the physiotherapy with a patience and sympathy at variance with the cool manner he demonstrated towards the hospital staff.

Sarah, left to herself for a time, got on with the morning's chores until Mrs Drew and Mrs Pearce arrived, and, hard on their heels, the first patients for the Surgical Outpatients; after that there was no time for anything but the work at hand until, one by one, they went along to the canteen for their coffee-break. As Sarah made her way back to her desk she could see the vast back of Professor Nauta, trailed by his registrar and a houseman, disappearing down the long corridor leading to the main hospital. He was walking fast and she felt a fleeting pity for his companions, who while trying to keep up with him were probably being treated to some of his impatient and caustic remarks.

The day, wet and windy as only March could be, darkened early. The clinics were finishing, Sarah and her companions had gone in turn to their cups of tea and, since there was nothing much to do, she had been left to deal with the telephone or any enquiries while they went to tidy themselves up so that, promptly at five o'clock, they could leave to catch their buses. Mrs Drew lived in Clapham and Mrs Pearce had a long journey each day to and from Leyton, and since Sarah had a room within ten minutes' walk of the hospital it had been taken for granted for some time now that she would be the last to leave. She cleared up, put things ready for the morning and went back to her desk to scan the appointments book. It was quiet now; the nurses had gone and so had the doctors, all but Professor Nauta, who had returned half an hour previously and gone to his consulting-room, pausing just long enough to tell her that on no account was he to be disturbed. She had just stopped herself in time from enquiring what she should do in case of fire or emergency. Leave him to burn to a crisp, neglect to inform him of some dire happening? He would never forgive her. She had murmured politely at his cross face and gone back to her work. And now, in five minutes or so, she would be free to go home.

The wide swing-doors, thrust open by a firm hand, caused her to look up in surprise. She eyed the elderly lady who was advancing towards her with a purposeful air, and said politely, 'I expect you've missed your way? This isn't a ward—just the outpatients' clinics. If you will tell me which ward you want, I'll show you the way.'

The visitor stood on the other side of the desk studying her. She was a handsome woman, and dressed with an elegance which whispered money discreetly. She put her handbag down on the desk and spoke. She had a clear, rather high voice and an air of expecting others to do as she wished. 'I wish to see Professor Nauta; perhaps you would be kind enough to tell him.'

Sarah eyed her thoughtfully. 'The Professor left instructions that on no account was he to be disturbed. I'm sorry—perhaps I could make an appointment for you?'

'Just let him know that I wish to see him...' She smiled suddenly and her whole face lit up with a faintly mischievous look.

Sarah lifted the receiver and buzzed the Professor's room. 'A lady is here,' she told him. 'She wishes to see you, sir.'

He said something explosive in what she took to be Dutch; it sounded forceful and very rude. 'Good God, girl, didn't I tell you that I wasn't to be disturbed?'

'Indeed you did, sir.' She was suddenly annoyed—she was, after all, only doing what had been asked of her by this rather compelling lady, and if he wanted to use bad language he wasn't going to be allowed to use it to her. 'You should watch your language,' she told him tartly, and was instantly appalled. She would get the sack . . .

'Tell him that I am his mother,' suggested the lady.

'Your mother wishes to see you, sir,' said Sarah, and thumped the receiver back without waiting for a reply.

The Professor, for all his size and bulk, could move swiftly and silently; he was looming over Sarah's desk before she could regain her habitual serenity.

Not that he had anything to say to her. A very rude, arrogant man, considered Sarah, watching him greet his parent with every appearance of delight, then escort her to his consulting-room without saying a word to herself. When Mrs Drew and Mrs Pearce returned within minutes, she got her things and left with them. Normally, she would have told whoever was on duty in the Lodge that the Professor was still there, but just for once she wasn't going to do that. Let him be locked in or want her for something; her hours were nine to five, on paper at least, and it was already ten minutes past the hour.

She walked back to her bedsitting-room, still put out. His mother could have said at once who she was and saved a good deal of unpleasantness. Now Sarah had been rude to a consultant and, if he chose to do so, he could get her fired. She walked briskly down the respectable, dull street of terraced houses and let herself into the end one, went up the shabby stairs, bare of carpet, and unlocked the door of her bedsit.

It was quite a large room, papered in a dreary green, its paintwork a useful dark brown, its low window opening on to a decrepit balcony with a corrugated roof. It was because of the balcony that Sarah stayed there; Charles, the cat she had befriended as a kitten, regarded it as his own and she had gone to a good deal of trouble to make it a home for him: there was grass growing in a pot at one end, a basket lined with old blanket, water and food, even a ball for him to toy with when he got bored. When she was home he joined her in the room, sat beside her while she ate her meals and slept on her feet. He came to meet her now and, as usual, she told him of her day's doings as she took off her things, hung them behind the curtain in one corner, and started to get their supper.

The room was furnished, after a fashion: there was a divan bed, a table, two chairs, a down-at-heel easy chair drawn up to a gas fire, some shelves along one wall and a small gas stove beside a sink. Sarah had done what she could to improve it with a cheerful bedspread, cushions and a cheap rug on the floor, flowers, even when she had to go without something in order to buy them, and a pretty reading-lamp. All the same, it was a far cry from her home in Kent. It was several years since she had left it and she was still homesick for the nice old house and the quiet country round it. But she had known long before she'd left home that she would have to go; her stepmother had never liked her, and when her father had died she had made it plain to Sarah that she had no longer been welcome in her home. That had been five years ago and Sarah, twenty-eight years old, thought it unlikely that she would ever go home again.

Nor for that matter, did she think that anything exciting would happen to her. She was in a rut, earning just enough to live on, knowing few people, too shy to join a club of any sort and painfully aware that the girls in other rooms of the house regarded her as rather dull—even if willing enough to lend tea and sugar and listen, upon occasion, to one of their highly coloured lamentations of a love-affair gone wrong. She was aware too that they pitied her for her lack of boyfriends and pretty clothes. She dressed nicely but always with an eye to long-lasting fashion, so that no one bothered to look at her twice.

As she pottered round the room, she talked to Charles. 'In a nasty temper, he was,' she pointed out as she scooped his supper into a saucer. 'I wonder what he's like at home? If he has a home... I just can't imagine anyone wanting to marry him. He's to be pitied... I wonder why his mother wanted to see him? It must have been something urgent.'

Charles, his furry face buried in his supper, took no notice. 'I'd quite like to know,' said Sarah to his uninterested back.

* * *

The Professor closed the door gently after his parent, offered her the chair behind his desk, then stood leaning back against the door, his hands in his pockets. 'Nice to see you, my dear. Something's worrying you?' He smiled as he spoke so that his stern expression became all at once attractive.

His mother settled herself comfortably. 'Who is that girl at the desk?'

His smile widened; his mother, a charming woman, had a mind which leapt from here to there, sometimes without obvious reason. 'The receptionist and clerk, one of three. Miss Sarah Fletcher.'

'She told you to mind your language...'

'So she did. I could get her sacked for that.'

'But you won't?'

'Of course not.'

'Your grandmother would like her.'

His eyes narrowed. 'Is that why you have come over to see me, Mama?'

She nodded. 'Yes, dear. Your father and I have talked about it and we decided that I should come and talk to you about her. She will be coming out of hospital in ten days' time; there's nothing more to be done for her, as you know, but she absolutely refuses to have a nurse—she says she has seen all the nurses she ever wishes to see. On the other hand, there must be someone to be with her... I wondered if you know of anyone? You see, your father feels that she has every right to do whatever she likes now that she has so short a time to live.' She paused. 'It struck me, just now waiting for you, that the young woman at the desk was just the type she would tolerate. And don't tell me I'm fanciful, it was one of my feelings...'

He left the door and perched on the edge of his desk. 'You think that Grandmother would be happy with her?'

'Yes, I do. I don't know anything about the girl, just this feeling in my bones... She looked kind and patient. Nothing to look at, of course, but Grandmother isn't going to mind about that.' She fetched a sigh. 'Your father is very worried—I know she is an irritable old autocrat, but she is his mother and she is ninety.'

'And she only has a few more weeks to live.' He frowned down at his beautifully polished shoes. 'If Miss Fletcher has some holidays due to her I might be able to persuade her to go over to Holland and stay with you. I don't imagine she travels around much; probably lives at home with her parents or goes home for her holidays.'

'She's not married or anything like that?'

'I wouldn't know, Mama. I can find out, of course. Have you been to my place yet? You left your baggage there? Good. Can you stay for a couple of days and I'll see her in the morning? I shall have to see the hospital manager if she agrees. She may refuse...'

His mother got to her feet. 'I'm being a nuisance, my dear. I'll get a taxi and leave you to finish whatever it was that you were doing.'

'I'll drive you home and come back after dinner. You will want to phone Father.'

He smiled at her very kindly and she wondered if he smiled at his patients like that. She suspected that he allowed no one but his family and close friends to see anything of his warmth and kindness; he was thirty-six now, she reflected, and it was ten

years since the girl he had intended to marry had
thrown him over for a South American millionaire.
Ever since then he had allowed no one and nothing
to get beneath his smooth, cold politeness.
Mevrouw Nauta, sending up a silent prayer that
someday soon a girl with enough love and deter-
mination would penetrate that chilly civility, followed her only son out of the room.

It was raining the next morning as Sarah bade
Charles goodbye and ran down the stairs. It would
be a busy day, she remembered, for Mrs Drew had
arranged to have a day off so that she could take
her small son to the dentist. She hung up her
dripping raincoat, smoothed her damp mass of hair
and sat down at her desk, ready to welcome the
first patient.

It was Mr Clew's morning and his patients, legs
in plaster, arms in slings, quite a few on crutches,
came pouring in. His clinic wasn't over until
lunchtime, when Mrs Pearce took herself off to the
canteen, leaving Sarah to get ready for the afternoon. Post-Natal and toddlers, and likely to go on
long after five o'clock. She ticked off names, arranged old notes where they could be got at a moment's notice and wondered what the canteen had
to offer in the way of a hot meal. For reasons of
economy her breakfast was frugal, and now her insides were rumbling.

The door, thrust open impatiently by Professor
Nauta, made her look up. Her heart sank, remembering that she had been impertinent on the previous day and he was probably going to tick her
off—or worse, threaten her with dismissal. She sat

up a little straighter in her chair and wished him a calm good morning.

'Have you had your lunch?' he wanted to know, not wasting time on niceties.

'No, sir.' She glanced at the clock. 'In ten minutes.' She folded her hands in her lap and waited for him to speak.

'Perhaps you will be good enough to have lunch with me?' And, at her look of absolute surprise, 'I wish to have a talk with you. I am a busy man and can spare little time and you, I imagine, have your work to do. I will be outside the main entrance in fifteen minutes' time.'

He had turned on his heel and gone through the doors before she had managed to close her astonished mouth and give utterance.

The idea that he was suffering from overwork and unaware of what he was doing crossed her mind, to be instantly denied—he wasn't that kind of man. There was no doubt in her mind that he had meant exactly what he had said. And where would they go for a meal? Surely not to the hospital canteen, that hotbed of gossip? She wasn't dressed for the type of restaurant he probably frequented, and, besides, why should he waste money on her? She gave up worrying about that and worried about why he wanted to see her, instead.

When Mrs Pearce came back from her own lunch, Sarah tidied herself, got into her raincoat and took herself off to the main entrance. Mrs Pearce hadn't been very punctual and it was several minutes past the fifteen he had told her. Perhaps he wouldn't be there... He was, sitting in his dove-grey Rolls-Royce, beating a tattoo on the steering-wheel.

It surprised her when he got out and went round the car to open the door for her, but she said nothing; only when she was sitting beside him she reminded him, 'I have three-quarters of an hour for lunch, Professor.'

'I am aware of that.' He drove out of the hospital forecourt into the busy East End and turned the car south towards the river. Just past the Monument he turned into a narrow street and stopped before a corner pub.

At her look he said smoothly, 'Perfectly respectable, Miss Fletcher; I come here frequently for lunch.'

He ushered her out of the car and in through the doors to a snug bar, almost empty of customers although from the other side of the passage Sarah could hear cheerful voices and the thud of darts on the dartboard.

She was urged to a corner table and asked what she would like to drink. Something to keep up the courage she felt sure she was going to need presently? Or tonic water and a clear head? She chose the latter.

'The beef sandwiches are excellent,' suggested the Professor, sounding almost friendly, and he gave the order, at the same time glancing at his watch. 'I shall not beat about the bush,' he told her and she nodded; she would have been surprised if he had.

'Do you have any holidays due to you?'

There seemed no point in asking him to explain at the moment. 'Yes, two weeks.'

'Good. Have you a family, Miss Fletcher? Parents, sisters, brothers?'

'No.'

'Then if you have no plans for your holiday would you consider going over to Holland and acting as companion to my grandmother? Ninety years old and extremely tetchy; she is also dying.' He broke off as the sandwiches were put on the table with her tonic water and his beer. 'I should perhaps tell you that my mother took an instant liking to you and feels that you are exactly the right person to be with my grandmother.'

Sarah eyed him cautiously. 'We barely spoke,' she pointed out calmly. 'It sounds a lot of double Dutch to me.' She stopped and went red. 'I am sorry, I quite forgot that you are Dutch.'

He inclined his head gravely and gave her a cool look down his commanding nose. 'Let us not concern ourselves with my feelings,' he begged. 'Be good enough to consider what I have said; we shall, of course, pay all expenses and a suitable fee, and all arrangements will be made for you. It would be convenient if you could travel within the week.'

'I doubt if I could get my holidays at such short notice.'

'That can also be arranged, Miss Fletcher.'

She bit into a sandwich. He was right, the beef was excellent. A sudden thought struck her as she took another bite. 'Oh, but I can't—I can't leave Charles.'

The Professor drank some beer. 'Charles? Your, er, young man?'

'I haven't got one,' she said flatly. 'Charles is my cat, and there is no one to look after him.'

He offered the sandwiches. 'I am on the committee of an animal sanctuary just across the river in Greenwich. Charles would be happy and well cared for there, and I will undertake to take him there and return him to you when you get back.'

She eyed him thoughtfully. 'You are going to a great deal of trouble, Professor Nauta.'

His eyes were cold steel. 'I am fond of my grandmother, Miss Fletcher.'

She finished her sandwich, drank the rest of her tonic water and sat back in the comfortable, shabby chair. She had nothing to lose, she reflected; it would make a delightful change from the drab respectability in which she lived, and he had said that Charles would be cared for. The fee would be welcome, too: shoes, a new dress for her meagre wardrobe, and perhaps, on a Bank Holiday, a daytrip to the sea. She heard herself say, 'Very well, Professor Nauta, if you will arrange everything and see that Charles is quite safe, I'll do it.'

She felt no last-minute regret, and as for the Professor, he showed no sign of satisfaction, merely nodded briefly and said, 'Thank you, Miss Fletcher. I will make the arrangements and keep you informed. Have you a passport?'

She shook her head.

'Then go to the post office and get a visitor's passport—it will be sufficient for your stay in Holland.' He glanced at his watch. 'We should be getting back.'

At the hospital he got out and opened her door. He said stiffly, 'My mother will be most grateful to you, Miss Fletcher. I am sure that you are no gossip, but I should be obliged to you if you will refrain from discussing our arrangement with anyone. The hospital manager will of course be in full possession of the facts.'

He got back into the car and drove away and she went back to her desk, five minutes late. It was unfortunate that the supervisor who headed the clerical staff was talking to Mrs Pearce. Miss Payne didn't like Sarah, and here was an opportunity to tick her off for being late.

'You mustn't make a habit of these slovenly ways,' said Miss Payne nastily. 'I haven't forgotten those three extra days you took with your last holidays on some trumped-up excuse. There are plenty of girls waiting to step into your shoes.'

Sarah didn't answer; indeed, she wasn't really listening, and Miss Payne turned back to Mrs Pearce, which left Sarah free to get ready for the afternoon's influx of patients while she thought about Professor Nauta's astonishing proposition. And what was more astonishing, she had agreed to it, and now that she had she felt excited. It would be wonderful to get out of the rut of her dull life for a couple of weeks; she began making plans as she ticked off names. She would raid the modest nest-egg in the bank and get some new clothes, something sensible that she could wear once the trip was over. There would be no need for anything other than blouses and skirts and a jacket; she would take her only decent dress to the cleaners on her way to work in the morning. Dove-grey wool jersey, timeless in its style and undoubtedly suitable.

The trickle of patients became a steady flow and then a flood and she had to call a halt to her plans.

* * *

It was two days before she had any further news of her trip. She had got herself a passport, washed and pressed and ironed, polished her elderly baggage, but she hadn't bought any clothes, not until she was quite certain... The Professor had taken his usual clinic, stalking past her desk without as much as a glance and, on his way out, accompanied by his registrar, he had paused briefly to say goodnight. Probably he hadn't meant a word of it, she told Charles as she got their suppers. 'And what a blessing I haven't bought any new clothes,' she observed rather crossly. 'Oh, well, we'll have to keep each other company, won't we?' She paused as she made the tea. 'And another thing—I wouldn't have taken two weeks' holiday at this time of year...'

There was an envelope on her desk the following morning. It contained flight tickets, instructions and the address of where she was going. She would be met at Schiphol, the Professor wrote in his crabbed handwriting, and she would find her expenses enclosed. He hoped that she would be agreeable to her fee's being paid weekly. The size of it sent her mousy eyebrows soaring. His granny must be a handful...

Her holiday had been allowed, and, if she would present herself at the hospital entrance at half-past seven on the following Saturday, a taxi would convey her to Heathrow. Charles would be fetched on Friday evening, and he trusted that she would consent to that. It was signed, without protestations of sincerity or faith, Radolf Nauta. Very businesslike, thought Sarah, but she hadn't expected anything less.

She put the envelope into her handbag in the drawer, and applied herself to the morning's work. Her holiday, by some lucky chance, was to start from noon on Friday—overtime, stated the slip she had had from the office—if she went without lunch and was lucky with buses she would be able to go to Oxford Street and replenish her wardrobe. Mrs Pearce and Mrs Drew wished her goodbye with ill-concealed curiosity. Sarah never went anywhere, not even on holidays, and beyond telling them that she would be going away she had said nothing. They settled back behind their desks when she had gone and speculated about it; they came up with any number of ideas, most of them far-fetched, but not as far-fetched as the truth.

Sarah got on a bus and took herself to Oxford Street, where she found herself a sensible pleated skirt in a useful shade of brown, a neat little jacket to go with it and a couple of drip-dry blouses. They did nothing to enhance her appearance, but they were suitable. A word she had come to loathe. Perhaps one day, she promised herself, her little nose very close to a shop window while she studied the latest fashions for the younger woman, she would take the whole of her nest-egg and spend the lot, and never mind the rainy day.

She hadn't been told who was to fetch Charles; she got out his shabby basket and put it ready, gave him an extra-special supper and sat down to wait. By eight o'clock no one had arrived, so she started to get her supper. 'And if no one comes,' she assured the animal, 'I shan't budge from here, so you don't need to worry.'

She was opening a can of beans when someone knocked on her door. The Professor stood there. 'I've come to collect Charles.'

She stood aside for him to squeeze past her. 'Good evening, Professor Nauta,' she said pointedly—quite lost on him, for he was examining her room with the air of a man who didn't find it to his taste.

'You live here?' he asked.

A silly question—she wished she could think of a silly answer. She said, 'Yes.' And then, remembering her manners, 'Will you sit down? Would you like a cup of coffee?'

'Thank you, no. I'm now on my way home; I'll hand Charles over as I go.'

She said urgently, 'You're sure he'll be all right? Properly looked after?'

'Quite sure.'

She picked up Charles, tucked him into his basket and fastened the lid, and he put a paw through the hole at the side and she held it for a moment. 'Be good,' she begged him. 'It's only for a little while.'

If the Professor hadn't been watching her with the faintest of sneers on his mouth, she would have wept; Charles was, after all, her companion in a lonely life. As it was, she closed her gentle mouth firmly and handed him the basket.

'I promise you that he will be most lovingly cared for,' said the Professor, surprising her, 'and when you return all you need to do is phone this number——' he gave her a slip of paper '—and he will be returned to you at once.'

She was lonely that night without Charles' portly form curled up at the bottom of the divan; it was a relief when she got up and had her breakfast and then got ready to leave. Mrs Potter, the landlady who lived in the basement, poked her head round the basement stairs to see her go. 'I'll keep your room, ducks!' she shouted, quite unnecessarily since Sarah had paid her rent for the two weeks she would be away. 'And 'ave a good time—meet a jolly bloke and 'ave some fun.'

Sarah thought it unlikely that there would be any jolly blokes near Granny. One never knew, of course; she fell into a pleasant daydream as she walked to the hospital: she would meet a man, handsome, rich, and he would fall instantly in love with her. It would be nice to go back to her bedsit a married woman, although of course if she married she wouldn't go back, would she? He would have to like cats...

The taxi was waiting for her. She wished the driver good morning, got in and was borne away to Heathrow and in due course found herself sitting—to her surprise—in a first-class seat of a KLM plane.

Accepting the coffee she was offered, she looked around her. Everyone else looked as though he or she flew to Schiphol every day as a matter of course—they even waved away the coffee in a bored kind of way and buried their noses in books. Sarah, who had never flown before, looked out of the window. There was nothing to see, only white and grey cloud; she wasn't sure that she felt quite safe, but it was an experience.

With the other passengers, she was processed through Schiphol, past Passport Control and Customs, who ignored both her and her case, and

finally into the vast hall filled with passengers
hurrying to and fro, coming and going with a confidence which made her feel suddenly a little scared.
Supposing no one met her? The Professor had
failed to give her a description of whoever it would
be—indeed, now she came to think about it, she
wasn't quite sure just where she was to go. There
had been nothing about that in the envelope,
although he had muttered some unintelligible name
when she had asked him. She stood where she had
been instructed to stand, by the enquiries desk, and
tried to look as though she knew what she would
be doing next.

The man who stopped in front of her was short
and stout, with a round face under a peaked cap.
It was a nice face, friendly and solid, and his little
blue eyes twinkled. 'Miss Fletcher? I am Mevrouw
Nauta's chauffeur, and if you will come with me I
will drive you to her house.'

He offered a hand and she shook it. 'Oh, you
speak English, I was wondering what I would do
if no one understood me.'

'English is spoken freely in Holland, Miss
Fletcher. If you will come?' He picked up her case
and led her outside to where an old-fashioned
Daimler, beautifully kept, was parked.

'May I sit with you?' asked Sarah. 'And will you
tell me your name?'

'Hans, miss.' He settled her in the front seat and
got in beside her. 'It is quite a long drive. I am
instructed to stop on the way so that you may have
coffee.'

He was driving away from the airport, and Sarah
said, 'I'm not quite sure where it is—where I am

to go. Professor Nauta told me, but it sounded a strange name and I didn't like to ask him again...'

'In the north, miss, just south of Leeuwarden—that is in Friesland.'

He had turned on to the motorway. 'We shall travel on the motorway for almost the whole way so that you will see little of Holland, and that is a pity, but perhaps before you go again you will have a chance.'

'You speak English very well.'

'I have lived in England, and I drive Mevrouw Nauta to see the Professor frequently.'

'Mevrouw Nauta is English?' She glanced at him. 'Please don't mind my asking questions; it would help me if I knew something of the people I am to work for.'

'She is English, miss, married to Mijnheer Nauta. He is also a physician, like his son, but now he works only at times. It is his mother whom you are to be with, I am told... An old lady, very old and very ill also. It is expected that she will die within a very short time, and she wished to be with her family.'

'The house—is it in the country?'

'Yes, by a small village, very quiet.' He sent the car speeding ahead. 'We circle Amsterdam, and travel north and across the dyke of the Ijsselmeer, but we will stop for coffee before we cross to Friesland.'

Sarah watched the outskirts of Amsterdam slip past. She didn't like to ask any more questions, but at least she knew where she was going. She settled down to enjoy the ride, although just for the moment there wasn't a great deal to see. But presently they left the city behind them, went through Purmerend and started on the stretch of motorway to Hoorn and the dyke, and Hans took care to point out everything which he thought might interest her as they went. They stopped at a pleasant restaurant only a few miles from the great sluice gates leading to the Afsluitdijk. Sarah asked Hans to have his coffee with her, and they spent a pleasant twenty minutes while he told her about his life in England, although he had nothing more to say about his employers.

On the *dijk* Sarah felt a pleasant excitement. She could see the land ahead of them, and in another half-hour or so they would be there. Supposing they didn't like her? Supposing Mevrouw Nauta's sudden wish to employ her had undergone a change? Supposing the old lady didn't like her? And that would be worse.

On land again, Hans cast her a sidelong look. 'No need to be nervous, miss. It is a happy family, and kind.'

Sarah, unable to imagine the Professor either particularly happy or kind, had her doubts.

They reached Franeker, and Hans turned off the road on to a narrow country road leading into a vista of flat green fields and small canals. Here and there villages, each with its vast church, were planted, screened by trees. He drove for several miles and the country changed, became more wooded, and in places there were glimpses of water.

'There are many lakes,' said Hans. 'These are very small, and beyond Sneek they are large and lead one to the other.'

They were nearing another village, its red roofs surrounding the church and ringed around by trees. 'Baardwerd,' said Hans. 'We have arrived.'

He drove through the tiny place and turned in through open gates and along a short drive. The house at the end of it was painted white, its many windows shuttered, and a double stairway led to its front door. Its roof was steep, with a clock over the wrought-iron balcony above the door. Sarah hadn't known what to expect; she had imagined several likely houses: red brick villas, a comfortable country house like her own home had been, even a narrow town house with a gabled roof. None of them as grand as this. She got out of the car, her heart beating rather too quickly from nerves.

CHAPTER TWO

WITH Hans close behind her, Sarah mounted the steps and found the door open and a tall, bony middle-aged woman standing there. The woman said something in Dutch and offered a hand, and Sarah took it gratefully as Hans said, 'This is my wife, Nel. She is housekeeper and speaks no English, but you will understand each other.'

Nel and Sarah smiled at each other hopefully as Hans opened the inner door of the lobby and ushered her into the hall. It was large and square with panelled walls and a very large chandelier hanging from the high ceiling. The black and white marble floor was exactly what anyone, having seen the pictures of Dutch interiors so often painted by the Dutch Old Masters, would have expected. The furniture was right, too: old chests, heavily carved, and massive armchairs capable of seating giants. Sarah followed Nel across the hall to the big double doors at one side, and was urged inside.

The room was just as vast as the hall, except there was no chandelier, only wall sconces and reading-lamps shaded in a delicate peach silk, and the furniture was a nice mixture of comfortable sofas and armchairs together with imposing display cabinets. The floor was carpeted and there was a fire burning under the hooded chimney-piece, so despite its grandeur it looked lived-in, almost homely.

Mevrouw Nauta got out of her chair by the fire as Nel stood aside and Sarah walked on alone.

'Miss Fletcher,' Mevrouw Nauta surged towards her and took her hand. 'I—we are delighted to see you and we are so grateful to you for giving up your holidays in order to help us.' She paused to say something to Nel, who went away. 'I'm sure you would like a cup of coffee... We lunch at half-past twelve, so there is just time for you to see your room and have a little chat. You must find all this very confusing, but I have these strong feelings and I always act upon them. I simply felt sure that you were exactly right for my husband's mother. She was brought back from hospital just an hour ago, and is resting quietly. You shall meet her presently——' She broke off as Nel came back with a young girl carrying a tray of coffee. 'Sit down, Miss Fletcher—must we call you that? Do you mind if we use your Christian name?'

'Sarah,' said Sarah. Mevrouw Nauta gave her the feeling that she was sitting in a strong wind—not unpleasant, but a bit overwhelming. She wondered fleetingly if the woman's son felt the same way, although if he had grown up with her he would be used to it. The door opened and a tall, elderly man came in, undoubtedly the Professor's father. He was white-haired and very slightly stooping, but had the same nose and blue eyes. Sarah, introduced, bade him a serene, 'How do you do?' and listened while he made her welcome. His voice was so like his son's that if she shut her eyes it could have been the Professor speaking...

'No sinecure,' he was saying. 'I hope Radolf made that clear. My mother is a fiery old lady even in these, the last days of her life. But I—and my son—have great faith in my wife's intuition; I feel sure that you will cope admirably. We are most grateful.'

She drank her coffee from paper-thin china, and presently was borne away by Nel. 'If you would like to unpack,' suggested Mevrouw Nauta junior, 'and return here, we will have lunch together before I take you to Mevrouw Nauta's room.' She hesitated. 'I think probably Radolf did not mention free time and so on? I thought not. I must warn you that, if Mevrouw Nauta takes a fancy to you, it will be necessary for you to take any time to yourself while she is resting—she sleeps a good deal but she is difficult to sedate, and day and night are much the same to her.'

Sarah followed Nel up the grand staircase, reflecting that, however difficult the old lady was, it was only for a fortnight, and with the extra money from her fees she would take herself off for a walking holiday weekend in the Cotswolds later in the year. And really, when she saw the room Nel ushered her into, she decided that she had no reason to quibble however difficult the old lady was. It was large and high-ceilinged, with two long windows and a door between them opening on to a balcony. The carpet underfoot was deep and soft, and the furnishings were in a restful mushroom-pink with pink patterned curtains and bedspread. The bed and dressing-table were in the style of Sheraton, and there was a dear little writing-desk between the windows and a small armchair drawn up to a reading-table. She had a brief vision of her bedsit in London—the contrast was cruel, and there

was no point in making it. She peeped into the
adjoining bathroom, which was peach-pink and
white, its fluffy towels, bowls of soap and bottles
of lotions calling forth a sigh of pleasure from her,
and then she started to unpack. It didn't take long;
she tidied herself and went down the staircase,
feeling nervous. Hans was in the hall, and he
ushered her into the drawing-room again. The
Nautas gave her a drink, and engaged her in gentle
talk until they crossed the hall to the dining-room,
where she sat between them at a large, round mahogany table, eating the delicious food before her
and keeping up her end of the conversation. After
they had had their coffee she was led back upstairs,
but this time they turned away from the gallery
which overlooked the hall and went down a wide
corridor. At a door halfway along it, Mevrouw
Nauta paused. 'I should have told you—it may be
necessary for you to stay up late or get up in the
night, so we have turned a small dressing-room next
to my mother-in-law's room into a bedroom for
you, so that if you think it necessary you can sleep
there and be at hand. We hope that there will be
no need of that; we do not expect you to stay with
her for twenty-four hours at a time, but as she grows
weaker...'

'I understand, Mevrouw Nauta—I won't leave
her if she wants my company.'

The room they entered was at the back of the
house overlooking the garden, which sloped away
in a vast sweep of lawn to a belt of trees. It was a
very large room and the small four-poster bed
against one wall was almost dwarfed by its size,
although it in its turn was dwarfing the tiny figure

lying in it. The Professor's grandmother was a very small lady, and frail. All the same, the eyes she turned on her visitors were still a vivid blue and her voice, a mere thread of sound, sounded decidedly ill-tempered.

Sarah didn't understand what she said, but then she switched to English, fluent but heavily accented. 'So you're the girl my son has decided I must have breathing down my neck. Well, my girl, I can't say I'm glad to see you, for I'm not. Come over here so that I can look at you.'

This is far worse than anything I had imagined, reflected Sarah, obligingly going to stand in a patch of sunlight. She stood still, looking a good deal calmer than she felt, and looked back at the cross face.

'Well, why did you come?' demanded the old lady.

'Because I was asked to.'

'You're being paid? Too much, I'll be bound.'

'Of course I'm being paid, Mevrouw; as to whether it's too much, I cannot say because I don't know.'

'Hmm—got a tongue in your head, too.' The blue eyes turned upon Mevrouw Nauta junior. 'Adele, go away while I talk to this girl.'

Mevrouw Nauta said something in a soothing tone and went away, and the old lady said briskly in her worn-out voice, 'Get a chair and come and sit by me. What's your name?'

'Sarah.' She sat obediently, and waited patiently while her companion closed her eyes and appeared to snooze for a few minutes.

'I'm dying, do you know that?'

'I have been told that you are very ill,' said Sarah cautiously.

'Have you met my grandson?'

'Yes. I work in the hospital where he is a consultant.'

'Like him?'

'I don't know him. I'm a clerk——'

'No looks to speak of,' muttered the old lady. 'Nice eyes, doesn't cringe, thank heaven. Give me a drink, Sarah.' The water revived her. 'Radolf isn't married.' She gave a naughty cackle of laughter. 'Setting your cap at him?'

Sarah laughed. 'Good gracious, no. He doesn't like me overmuch, you know, and I only work at the clinic where he's the consultant. I think perhaps you don't quite understand—we don't move in the same circles.'

'No looks, but not dim either,' said Mevrouw Nauta senior. 'I like to be read to. Late at night when everyone else is asleep.' She stared at Sarah. 'Did they tell you that? That I like company during the small hours? Not that you'll have to put up with that for long. If I don't like you, I shall say so.'

'Very sensible,' agreed Sarah pleasantly. 'Would you like me to read to you now?'

'Yes. *Jane Eyre*, over there on that table by the window. My daughter-in-law has been reading it to me, and it's almost finished. I'll have *Pride and Prejudice* next, not that there will be time to read it to the end.'

Sarah had fetched the book and opened it at the marker.

'Do you know how old I am?'

'Yes, Mevrouw Nauta, ninety.'

'The Nautas live long lives, but of course we none of us can go on forever.'

'I don't suppose that would be very pleasant,' agreed Sarah, and she began to read. She had a pleasant, very clear voice, and she read steadily until she glanced up and saw that the old lady was asleep. She put the marker back in the book and walked over to the window and looked out. The garden was quite beautiful and it was very quiet—after the noise and bustle of London it was bliss. But she doubted if she would have much opportunity to enjoy it. It seemed to her that she was expected to spend her days and nights with the old lady, with only the briefest of respites when it was convenient. But this gloomy outlook was quite wrong. Just before four o'clock, while the old lady still slept, Mevrouw Nauta came back.

'There has been little time to talk,' she observed. 'You must be thinking that we intended leaving you here for the rest of the day. I always have my tea up here, so you will be free for an hour at least. Then, if you will come back until just before eight o'clock, while you have dinner my mother-in-law's maid will make her ready for the night—that takes about an hour. It is then that I must ask you to take over until Mevrouw Nauta goes to sleep; she likes to be read to, and she loves to talk although it exhausts her. If she falls asleep around midnight, then she will not wake before six o'clock or later, but if she has a bad night then I am afraid I must ask you to sleep in the dressing-room…' She looked rather anxiously at Sarah. 'I think that Radolf didn't make all this quite clear to you? I thought not. During the day someone will relieve you for an hour or two so that you may feel free to do as you like. There is a pool in the garden if you like to swim and books in the library, and the village is close by. Of course, if her condition worsens, you may have to stay with her for longer periods. We shall do our best to make it up to you later. Now, do go and have your tea—you will find it in the drawing-room—and then take a stroll round the garden. There will still be time for you to change for the evening before you come back here.'

Thank heaven for the dove-grey, thought Sarah, agreeing pleasantly to everything her companion had said.

She had her tea with the master of the house, who put himself out to be pleasant. 'You know Radolf?' he asked her.

'No,' said Sarah, 'not really. I see him from time to time, that's all. I think he might not recognise me away from my desk at the hospital.'

Her host looked vaguely surprised and began to talk about the weather, a safe subject, and presently he offered to show her round the garden. It was much larger than she had thought; if she could spend an hour each day wandering in it she would be quite happy. She admired the flower-beds and, had she but known it, delighted her companion by showing a knowledge of the shrubs and trees around them.

'You have a garden?'

'No, I live in the East End of London, but my home is—was—in the country and we had rather a nice garden there; not as large as this one, but very pretty.'

She went to her room, showered and changed into the grey dress, and then went back to the old lady. She was as cross as two sticks, and Mevrouw Nauta junior looked harassed and lost no time in making off, leaving Sarah to pacify her elderly companion as best she could.

'Shall I read to you?' she asked hastily. 'Or shall we talk?'

'We will talk, young woman—at least, I shall talk and you will listen.'

So Sarah sat down by the bed and listened to the old lady talking of her earlier life. Every now and then she dropped off into a light doze, to wake refreshed and talk of her youth in a breathy voice, sometimes so faint that Sarah could hardly hear it.

After dinner, taken in the magnificent dining-room, sitting between the Nautas at a table glistening with silver and crystal, Sarah went back again, a little tired by now, and listened to the thin old voice until the old lady slept. It was almost midnight and the house was quiet; she arranged the bell where it could be reached should Mevrouw Nauta senior wake and want her, and went to her room, undressed and got into bed, rather worried at the idea of leaving the old lady alone, but reassured by the bell on the bedside table. Her own bed was blissfully warm and comfortable, and she slept within minutes.

Within the next two or three days she achieved some kind of a flexible routine, although this depended very much on Mevrouw Nauta's state of health. That she was going downhill was obvious, despite the cheerful doctor who visited her each day. She had no appetite, and Sarah spent a good deal of time coaxing her to eat the dainty little dishes which the cook sent up. It was halfway through the week when Sarah, listening to her companion's half-whispered ramblings, discovered that she had been something of a pianist in her younger days. 'Girls don't play the pianoforte these days,' grumbled old Mevrouw Nauta.

'Well, I do,' said Sarah. 'Or at least, I did.' A remark which bore unexpected consequences, for when Sarah got back from her tea that afternoon there was a piano installed in one corner of the room.

'The schoolroom is on this floor,' explained the younger lady, 'and my mother-in-law told me that you played. It seemed a good idea to have the piano moved in here.'

So Sarah spent the evening and the succeeding days playing the tunes the old lady fancied, a state of affairs which pleased them both.

At the end of the week, Sarah began to feel that she had been there forever. St Cyprian's seemed of another world and, despite her erratic hours and lack of much free time, she was happy. The Nautas were kind to her and so were the servants; she couldn't understand them, of course, nor they her, apart from Hans. But he beamed goodwill, and they saw that there were flowers in her room and trays of tea the moment she had any spare time to herself. She even began to think that the old lady was improving—a mistake, as it turned out, for that very evening her peevishness made it impossible to settle her for the night. She declared that she had no intention of sleeping and that Sarah was to stay with her. 'And that's what you're paid for,' she pointed out waspishly.

'Of course I'll stay with you, but if you don't mind I'll go and have a shower and get into a dressing-gown first. Give me ten minutes,' begged Sarah, and whisked herself off to her room. It was still early; as she passed the head of the staircase she could hear voices downstairs, and Hans crossed the hall below. She was back with the old lady presently, cosily wrapped in the dressing-gown over her nightie, hopeful that in a little while Mevrouw Nauta might go to sleep and she could go to bed herself in the dressing-room.

The old lady had other ideas—Sarah played the piano with her foot on the soft pedal until after midnight, and then, obeying the ill-tempered old voice, started on chapter three of *Pride and Prejudice*. The clock was striking one o'clock when she was told to put the book down and play the piano again. 'And don't start on any of your lullabies,' said the irascible old lady, 'for I won't be soothed, I intend to stay awake all night.' So Sarah, thundering her way through some of Brahms' more dramatic works, her foot well down on the soft pedal again, didn't hear the door open, nor did she see Professor Nauta come into the room.

He glanced at his sleeping grandmother and crossed the room soundlessly. 'What the devil do you think you're doing?' he wanted to know, bending his vast person to reach Sarah's ear.

Sarah stopped in mid-bar, and swung round to face him. She had gone pale with fright and her voice was a furious squeak. 'How dare you frighten me? And you should watch your language, Professor.'

He stood towering over her, studying her small person wrapped cosily in her sensible woolly dressing-gown. Her hair, which she had plaited ready for bed if she was lucky enough to get to it, had come loose and hung in a shining mass almost to her waist, and her eyes were heavy with sleep.

He put a gentle hand on her shoulder. 'I'm sorry, I think I was surprised—it was hardly what I expected.'

She was very conscious of his hand. 'Your grandmother is having a bad night, and she wanted me to play for her. Why are you here?' She caught her breath. 'I'm sorry, it's your home, I didn't mean to be rude.'

'To say goodbye,' he said softly. 'It will be only a few more days now.' He turned his head and looked across to the bed, his face suddenly relaxed and smiling. Sarah looked too—old Mevrouw Nauta was awake.

The Professor crossed the room and sat down on the side of the bed. He took his grandmother's hand in his and bent to kiss her cheek, and then began a cheerful conversation in his own language. Presently he turned his head. 'Go to bed, Sarah,' and, as she started towards the dressing-room, 'No, not there, your own room. I'm going to stay and talk to my grandmother. I'm not in the least tired. There is coffee in the kitchen—do you know where that is? Have a drink and go to bed; you will be called in the morning.'

She made a feeble protest, but she was tired and tomorrow would be another long day. She had her coffee, had a quick shower, got into bed and was asleep within seconds.

When she woke up the Professor was sitting on the edge of her bed, balancing a small tray with two mugs on it. She shot up in bed, peering at him through a curtain of hair. 'Mevrouw Nauta—she's worse? I must get up——'

'Presently. Drink your tea first. She is no worse. There's no one up yet—it's not yet six o'clock, but she has a fancy for a little music. I told her she would have to wait just a few minutes while I fetched you from your bed.'

Sarah gulped her tea. The Professor looked weary and he needed a shave. 'You must go to bed,' she told him in a no-nonsense voice. 'I'll get dressed.'

'Come as you are. Put on your dressing-gown and slippers and play anything she fancies—she is on the edge of sleep, and you will have time to dress and breakfast shortly.' He got off the bed, fetched her dressing-gown from a chair and picked up the tray. 'Don't waste time,' he begged her.

So she pattered along to the old lady's room, bade her good morning and sat down at the piano.

'Schubert,' ordered her companion in a wispy voice, 'and then Delius. When is my supper coming?'

'Very soon,' said Sarah in her quiet voice. 'I'll play until it does, shall I?'

Ten minutes later the Professor came again, this time bearing another tray with a small jug and glass. He had found time to shave and change into a sweater and slacks, and he no longer looked tired. Sarah wondered how he did it. She allowed her fingers to wander through *Rosamunde* while her thoughts wandered too. It had been a strange night; she had never known one like it, and most likely never would again. When she got back to the hospital, sitting at her desk soberly ticking off names, and remembered this night, she felt sure she wouldn't believe it. She tossed her hair back impatiently and felt the Professor's hands gathering it into a cascade and plaiting it. 'That's better,' he said. 'Not so distracting.' He gave a little laugh and went back to sit by the bed...

Half an hour later the old lady was asleep and he got to his feet. 'She will sleep soundly for a couple of hours at least. Get dressed and have your breakfast, and we'll see how things are.'

'You should go to bed,' she reminded him, closing the piano thankfully.

'Your concern on my behalf flatters me but is quite unnecessary, Sarah. Go and dress.'

Once or twice during that strange night she had caught herself almost liking him—now she wasn't so sure. She went ahead of him with something of a flounce and didn't answer.

The day turned out to be almost as strange as the night had been. The old lady was becoming confused—she refused to believe that it was morning and presently, with the blinds drawn, fell into a restless sleep. Sarah sat quietly, watching the small figure in the bed. People came and went: the Nautas, the Professor, and then Nel with coffee for Sarah. She had just finished it when the Professor returned.

'Go and take a turn in the garden,' he told her. 'I'll be here, so don't argue—when my grandmother wakes again you'll have your hands full.'

Which turned out to be very true. Old Mevrouw Nauta, refreshed by her sleep, demanded supper once again, dismissed her grandson and insisted on more music. Sarah played for some time, and would have stopped for a while but she was urged to continue, so that it was well after lunchtime when the Professor came once more into the room. 'Off with you,' he told Sarah. 'Lunch is ready for you.'

She said quickly, 'I can't—Mevrouw Nauta has just told me to go on playing.'

'She will have to put up with me.' He scooped her off the stool and took her place, and much to her surprise began to play Debussy. He took no notice of her, and his grandmother had her eyes closed; she went downstairs and ate her lunch and then, urged by Mevrouw Nauta junior, took a walk in the garden. When she went back, the Professor and his grandmother were talking softly together and he had her hand in his. He got up presently and went away with nothing but a casual nod.

The following two days and nights followed the same erratic pattern so that Sarah hardly knew what time of day it was, but old Mevrouw Nauta was quieter now, content to lie and listen to Sarah playing and from time to time reading out loud. Sarah had company for a good deal of the time: Mevrouw sat quietly in a corner of the room, knitting or embroidering, and her husband wandered in and out to sit by the bed and listen to his mother, rambling a little now but still chatty and occasionally querulous.

It was the Professor who shared the long hours of the night with Sarah and the old lady, sitting relaxed by the bed while Sarah played or read aloud

or sat thankfully silent while he and his grandmother talked. He made the old lady laugh, a weak
chuckle which Sarah found pathetic, and he
brought her flowers, delicate little nosegays which
Sarah arranged in vases around the room. Always
he behaved as though his grandmother were well,
ignoring her confusion, discussing the new flower-
beds in the garden that his father was having dug,
just as though she would be there to see them when
they were planted, coaxing her to eat and sometimes drawing Sarah into their conversation,
slipping back into English, never at a loss for the
cheerful talk the old lady enjoyed.

It was four o'clock in the morning of the third
day when the old lady closed her eyes and didn't
wake again. Sarah had been reading to her while
the Professor lounged in a chair by the bed, his
eyes on his grandmother. Something made her look
up, and she faltered and stopped and then closed
the book. She drew a sharp breath, and wishing
not to intrude, whispered, 'Oh, she ... what do you
want me to do?'

He picked up the small hand on the coverlet and
kissed it. 'Nothing, Sarah. My mother and father
came this evening while you were in your own room,
and so did the servants. I'll fetch Nel presently. Go
to bed now.'

'I can't leave you alone ...'

He turned to look at her, and she was shocked
at the grief in his calm face. 'Do as I say, Sarah.'

So she went, to lie awake for a time and then fall
into the sleep she needed so badly. She woke once,
to remember that she was due back at work in two
days' time. When she woke the second time it was

to find Nel standing by the bed with a breakfast tray. There was a note propped up against the teapot telling her that the family hoped that she would join them for coffee, but that if she was still tired she was to remain in bed.

She went downstairs presently and found Mevrouw Nauta in the drawing-room. Her husband was there too, but there was no sign of the Professor. 'Radolf has gone to make the necessary arrangements,' Mevrouw Nauta told her. 'He should be back at any moment. You slept? You have had a tiring two weeks, my dear, and we are most grateful to you.'

'You made my mother very happy,' observed Mijnheer Nauta. 'She loved music, above all the piano.'

When the Professor joined them he said at once, 'My grandmother asked that you should attend her funeral, Sarah. In four days' time. I'll arrange for you to travel back the day after that.'

'Well,' said Sarah, 'I don't think——'

She was stopped by his frown. 'It was her particular wish—unless you have any other plans?'

She bristled at his manner—indifferent and arrogant, she told herself, and she was on the point of reminding him that her plans included going back to work when Mevrouw Nauta chimed in. 'Oh, do please stay, Sarah, you were so good to her and it was her wish.'

'Very well,' said Sarah quietly, and listened politely while Mevrouw Nauta enumerated the family who might be expected to attend the funeral. Sarah hoped that there weren't many more like the Professor.

She wrote to the head of her department that afternoon. Miss Payne disliked her, but surely she would understand that Sarah couldn't refuse to stay in Holland? She walked to the village, very glad to be free to go where she liked, purchased a stamp and posted her letter—happily unaware that there was a lightning strike of postmen in England, and that the chances of her letter's getting to its destination on time were slim.

The next three days were extremely pleasant. She had her meals with the family and spent some time with Mevrouw Nauta, but the rest of the days were hers. She wandered around the countryside and on the second day borrowed a bike and went further afield. The weather was kind, for at least it didn't rain, and on the third day she cycled the seven miles over to Sneek. She hadn't the time to see much and she longed for time to explore, but at least she had seen one Dutch town.

Of the Professor there was little to be seen; he was polite to her when they met at meals, but she had the feeling that he was avoiding her. That, she supposed, was natural enough—he had engaged her to be a companion to his grandmother, and now she was surplus to his requirements. He was polite at the funeral, introducing her, when their paths crossed, to the hordes of family and friends who came. Sarah shook hands and murmured politely, lost in a sea of strange faces.

It wasn't until that evening at dinner that she heard him telling his parents that he would be leaving that night. It seemed that they already knew that he was going away, but now for some reason he would be going almost at once.

'You'll take the car?' asked his father, and nodded his head when the Professor observed that it was an easy drive.

He bade her goodnight and hoped that she would have a good journey, his voice so cold that she replied stiffly in as few words as possible. It was Hans, driving her to Schiphol the following morning, who told her that the Professor had gone to Germany for a fortnight. 'He lectures, miss, and he'll call in on his way back to London, I expect.' He added, 'We are all quite sorry to see you go, miss. You made the old lady's last days very happy.'

She thanked him gratefully, responding suitably to his hope that they would meet again at some time, and said goodbye at Schiphol with regret.

The Professor might not like her overmuch, but he had arranged her journey meticulously. Moreover, he had arranged for someone to deliver Charles to her bedsit that evening, for which she was grateful, for without her cat her homecoming would have been lonely indeed. Her room, after the luxury of the Nautas' home, seemed smaller and darker and shabbier than it actually was, but once the fire was lit and Charles had settled down in front of it and she had unpacked her few things, her good sense reasserted itself. She had a home, even though it was one room, and she had a job, too.

She was at her desk in good time in the morning, confident that Miss Payne, however much she disliked her, would have accepted her letter. Besides, the Professor, when he arranged her return, would surely have explained why she hadn't gone back to her job when she should have done.

An hour later she was forced to admit that he had either forgotten or had decided it wasn't necessary to give any explanation to her department. Miss Payne, choosing her time between clinics, had come to see her and hadn't minced her words. Sarah was not to be depended upon, and was she aware that this was the second time that she had returned late from a holiday without bothering to let anyone know?

'But I wrote you a letter,' objected Sarah.

'Stuff and nonsense—there has been no letter. That is the easiest excuse to make, for I have no means of knowing if you are speaking the truth.'

'Then you are a very silly woman,' declared Sarah. She wished she hadn't said that the moment the words popped out, for Miss Payne had gone a dull red and her already thin mouth had practically disappeared, but, a normally mild-tempered girl, Sarah was now extremely cross. If only the Professor had been in the hospital, she could have referred Miss Payne to him, but he wasn't.

She sat looking at Miss Payne, who was ugly in her wrath, and wondered what would happen next. At least Mrs Pearce and Mrs Drew were having their coffee and there were no patients around.

'Don't imagine that this is the end of the matter,' snapped Miss Payne and stalked away, still red in the face, her back like a ramrod.

It wasn't two days later that there was a letter for Sarah. Certain changes were being made, and a number of posts were being made redundant. She was to leave at the end of the week with a week's pay in lieu of notice.

—

CHAPTER THREE

SARAH read the letter through twice, put it back in its buff envelope and considered what was best to be done. She could of course seek out Miss Payne and try and explain, but the Professor had said when he had first asked her to go to Holland that he didn't want it to be talked about, and she could hardly blame him for forgetting that she should have been back at work several days before he had arranged her return trip. Besides, she should have made it clear that she had to return on time. Mrs Pearce and Mrs Drew were sympathetic but not helpful, only too thankful that they still had their jobs, and when Sarah asked for a reference she was given one which damned her with faint praise: a good worker, but unreliable...

She left at the end of the week; she had a little money saved and there would surely be a suitable job somewhere in London. By the end of the first week she had to admit that she had had very little success—even when she had got as far as an interview, her reference was the stumbling block. The fact that she had worked at the hospital for a number of years carried no weight in the face of unreliability. She spent a second week applying for any clerical job she could find, but still with no success. She was told that she was too old, unable to use a computer, a word processor...

Dispirited, but by no means beaten, she took herself into a small café and ordered a pot of tea, and while she drank it she worked out her finances. They were getting low—something would have to be done. She poured a last cup of tea and picked up a copy of *The Lady* magazine which someone had left on the table. There was nothing under the heading of clerical workers. She read the adverts for nannies with regret—she liked babies and children, but she couldn't with the wildest stretch of imagination call herself experienced. She fell to reading the domestic situations vacant; there were several pages and, by the time she had read the first page, she knew what she was going to do. Here was a market, almost untapped from the look of it, and she was perfectly able to clean a house, wait at table and answer a door. It would have to be somewhere where Charles would be welcome. She began to read more carefully, marking the most likely adverts.

She wrote six letters that evening to the six most promising offers. Each of them stressed the urgency of getting help and she surmised that, if that was really the case, Charles might be allowed to accompany her. To her surprise and delight, all six replied. She sifted through them carefully; they all agreed to her taking her pet, but only one offered a small cottage close to the house where she might live.

A country estate, said the letter, on the outskirts of a small village south of Bedford. She would be required to undertake the duties of housemaid and, when necessary, wait at table. The house was adequately staffed, but the staff were elderly; it must be understood that she must be prepared to help wherever help was needed. Her cat was welcome, provided that he was well trained. The wages seemed to her to be more than satisfactory, and she would have a day off each week. References would be required and she might attend an interview at Duke's Hotel, Knightsbridge should she consider the post, bringing three references with her. The interview was for the following day.

Sarah dressed in the grey jersey dress, her abundant hair smoothed into a chignon, and presented herself at the appointed time. There were several other young women there, all, she supposed, with impeccable references, whereas she had only those from the rector at home and the family doctor, and Miss Payne's letter with its subtle hint of unsatisfactory conduct.

The three who went in ahead of her came out looking pleased with themselves, and there were two more going in after her. She wasn't hopeful—still less so when she saw the elderly lady sitting beside a table by the window in the luxurious hotel room.

'Sit down.' The lady had a commanding voice. 'There, facing the window.' And when Sarah had sat, 'Your name is Fletcher, Sarah Fletcher? Why do you want to work for me?' She glanced at Sarah's letter. 'You say here that you are a clerical worker.'

'I have been made redundant, I can't find similar work and I need a job.'

'Why were you made redundant?'

'I returned three days late from my holiday. Last year I came back a day late.'

'You had good reasons for doing so?'

'Yes.'

'You are twenty-eight—do you intend to remain in domestic service for the rest of your working life? You have no—er—relationships?'

'No family, and I'm not engaged or living with anyone.'

The lady nodded. 'I see. You will be notified as to the result of this interview within the next day or two, Miss Fletcher. Thank you.'

Sarah went back to her room and wept all over Charles, who licked his damp fur dry and eyed her reproachfully—he wanted his supper. Sarah opened a tin of cat food and put a sausage roll on a plate for herself. Waiting for the kettle to boil on the gas ring, she wondered out loud where the Professor was and what he was doing. 'It's a waste of time thinking about him,' she observed to Charles. 'He doesn't like me, and by now he'll have forgotten that I ever existed. Besides, he's ill-tempered and impatient. I shall forget him.'

She bit into her sausage roll with a defiant snap.

She paid her rent the next morning and wondered uneasily how many more weeks she would be able to afford it. She could write to her stepmother, something she hadn't done for several years, but she would have to be desperate indeed. She wondered if she should have mentioned the fact that she had a stepmother when she had been interviewed. But that lady wasn't family—indeed, she had expressed a wish never to set eyes on Sarah again, and Sarah was sure that she would refuse any financial help if she were asked for it. There was the Social Security, of course, but that would be the very last resort. Sarah told herself bracingly not to have any gloomy thoughts.

The letter came the following morning: her references were satisfactory, and she was to convey herself and her cat to Bedford, where she would be met and taken to Shotley Park. She was expected on the following day, and the train arriving at Bedford at three o'clock was to be taken.

Sarah read the letter slowly, did a joyful dance around the room with Charles tucked under her arm and went to see her landlady. It was a pity she had just paid a week's rent but, as she had expected, it would be kept in lieu of a week's notice.

'Goin' somewhere nice?' asked Mrs Potter.

'Right away from London,' said Sarah, and she didn't say where. 'May I leave my big case in your box-room and send for it later? I can't manage more than one case if I've got Charles and his basket.'

'Just so long as it's only for a week or two, otherwise I'll have to charge,' cautioned Mrs Potter. 'You're going a bit sudden like, I'll have to re-let...'

Sarah murmured consolingly, knowing that Mrs Potter would let her room the moment she and Charles were out of the way.

She packed a case, filled another with her few bits and pieces, hauled it along to the communal box-room, washed her hair and went to bed. The die was cast—or should it be dye? she wondered.

The journey to Bedford took just a little over an hour. She tucked Charles in his basket discreetly away under her seat, and since the carriage was almost empty no one noticed him. At Bedford she got out and walked slowly to the barrier, not knowing who to expect. She was impressed when a uniformed chauffeur standing by the ticket collector touched his cap and asked if she was Miss Fletcher.

'I'm Lady Wesley's chauffeur, Knott. I'm to take you to an outfitter's to collect your uniform before I drive you to Shotley Park.'

He took her case and she put Charles, mute and dignified in his basket, on to the back seat of the Jaguar and got into the front seat, and the chauffeur drove off at once.

Sarah sat silently, not quite sure how to behave. Was a housemaid low in the hierarchy of domestic service and, if so, should she wait to be addressed before she spoke? It seemed that she should. Knott gave her a sideways look, liking what he saw. Quiet little thing—knew her place, too. Mrs Legge, the housekeeper, would be glad of that. He said, very slightly pompously, 'The outfitter's is in the high street. You're to collect your parcels and say who you are.'

'Very well, thank you, Mr Knott.' She heaved a hidden sigh of relief because she could see by his face that she had said the right thing.

There were several packages, but Knott got out of the car and put them in the boot and, when she got in beside him again, he said, 'It's about seven miles. I dare say you could do with a cup of tea.'

The country was pleasant, open and wooded here and there, and presently Knott turned in between imposing gates and drove slowly along a curving drive until the house came in sight. It was a good deal more imposing than Sarah had imagined it would be. There would be plenty of dusting and hoovering for her, she reflected, and it would take a long time to answer the door if one happened to be at the back of the mansion or even on the first floor. They drove round the side of the house and stopped in front of a side door set in a stone wall pierced by narrow windows. The house, Palladian from the front, was a complexity of outbuildings at its back where the house itself, the oldest part, was a maze of gables atop of a rambling wing surrounding a courtyard on two sides.

'Go in, then,' said Knott, not unkindly. So Sarah, taking Charles' basket and her courage in both hands, went in.

There was a stone passage leading to a vast kitchen, the floor there flagstoned too, its walls lined with cupboards and dressers, a large wooden table in its centre and an outsize Aga facing the door, flanked by more cupboards. An extremely stout woman was standing at the table carving a ham with a wicked-looking knife. She paused long enough to say, 'You're to go straight through to Mrs Legge's sitting-room. Through that door.'

Mrs Legge was sitting beside a cosy little fire, and a small table drawn up to her chair held an array of account books and a sheaf of bills. She put down her pen as Sarah knocked and went in, and looked at her, eyeing her case and Charles in his basket up and down.

'Sarah Fletcher?' she asked briskly.

'Yes, Mrs Legge.' Sarah stood patiently, waiting to hear what came next. Mrs Legge looked severe but not unkind. Sarah hoped that she liked cats, and was relieved when the housekeeper said, still brisk, 'You have the end cottage in the row opposite the kitchen door. Take your things there and come back to the servants' hall for your tea. Have you food for your cat?'

Sarah said that yes, thank you, she had, and went back the way she had come and out into the courtyard. Sure enough, there was the row of cottages facing her. They weren't really cottages—she suspected that at one time they had been a storage barn which had been converted, for there were four doors with four windows, a slate roof and a number beside each door. Presumably she was number four; she turned the handle and found the door open, the key in the lock on the inside. Inside, it was a great deal nicer than she had hoped: the room was small, furnished simply with a divan bed against one wall, but through another door was a very cramped shower-room and loo, and still another door opening on to a minute sink, a set of shelves and a gas ring. And, best of all, there was a door leading to an enclosed yard used by all four cottages, with a clothes-line, a wooden seat and a neglected flower-bed against the end fence. Sarah put down her case and let Charles out of his basket. He cringed a little—after years on his balcony, seemingly he was suspicious of so much open ground. Sarah picked him up and carried him as far as the fence and pointed out the flower-bed, pleased to see that he understood exactly what she meant. Presently he followed her back into the little cottage, ate the tea she put out for him and settled down on the divan. She went back to the house once more, very neat in her blouse and skirt, not a hair out of place.

There was no one in the kitchen and she stood irresolute until Knott put his head round the door at the far end. 'In here,' he told her, and added, 'It's all a bit strange—you will soon settle down.'

She smiled at him, grateful for his heartening words, and following him went into the servants' hall. Quite a comfortable room, she saw, with a long table down its centre with chairs all round it, and a couple of armchairs by the open fire. There was a piano in one corner and a dartboard on a wall, as well as a large TV dominating one end of the room.

She stood, uncertain where she should sit. Her own home hadn't been a grand house, but it had had its complement of servants and she remembered how strictly the hierarchy of the domestic world was obeyed.

'You'll sit there,' said Mrs Legge from the head of the table, 'next to Parsons, our parlourmaid, and that's Molly the kitchen maid on your other side.'

Sarah sat, greeted her neighbours politely, accepted a cup of very strong tea and a slice of bread and butter, cut thickly and lavishly spread, and waited to be spoken to.

'You're to be taken to Lady Wesley at six o'clock sharp,' said Mrs Legge. 'You'll change into uniform, Fletcher, and Parsons will take you round the house afterwards. You'll start work at half-past six tomorrow morning, and I'll see you after breakfast in my room.'

Sarah said, 'Yes, Mrs Legge,' and ate her bread and butter, and after a while the elderly man at the end of the table whom she took to be the butler asked her where she had been in service before.

A tricky question. 'Quite a small house in the country,' she told him. 'Well, a manor house, only three staff.' She paused, remembering the elderly cook, and old Nick, who did all the odd jobs as well as the garden, and Becky, who wasn't quite as bright as she should have been. Her stepmother had tried hard to get rid of them, but her father hadn't allowed it, and when he'd died Sarah had been delighted to discover that he had left each of them some money, enough to soften the blow of their discharge. She sent them a Christmas card each year and they always remembered her birthday...

'You were happy there?'

'Yes...' She hesitated, and Mr Cork saved her from thinking up the right answer by observing pompously, 'Well, I dare say you wished to improve yourself. This is a well-run household, as you will quickly discover for yourself. We are understaffed, but you look to be a sensible young woman. I hope you are strong.' He eyed her small, too thin person with some doubt, and she made haste to assure him that she was very strong and not easily tired.

He nodded and passed his cup for more tea, and she ate a second slice of bread and butter before he said a lengthy grace and everyone got to their feet.

Lady Wesley was in her sitting-room checking the household accounts with a sharp eye. She trusted her servants, but like so many well-to-do people she was inclined to meanness—certainly she liked to know where every penny went. She nodded to the housekeeper to go, took off her reading glasses and put on a pair of large hornrimmed ones, and studied Sarah.

'You appear smaller—I suppose it is the uniform.' Unexpectedly she smiled. 'You think you will like to work here? I must remind you that it will be in a menial capacity.'

'I am very glad to have a job, Lady Wesley. And I'm grateful to you for allowing me to have Charles with me. I'm sure I shall be happy here, and I will work as hard as possible.'

'And the staff? You think that you will get on well with them? You are not quite from the same background.'

'Well, no. I don't suppose that I shall work nearly as well as they do—they're professionals, as it were, aren't they? But I shall do my best.' She smiled. 'They were very kind to me at tea.'

'Well, we will hope for the best. You may go, Fletcher. You will take your orders from Mrs Legge, unless any member of the family wishes you to do something for them.'

Sarah said, 'Yes, Lady Wesley,' and took herself out of the room and back to the housekeeper's room, where she was given a list of her duties. 'And you may go with Parsons and turn down the beds and ready the bedrooms for the night. On her evenings off you will do that on your own, so make sure that you know what has to be done.'

There wasn't a great deal to do. Lady Wesley was a widow, and, although at weekends there were usually guests, during the week the big house was empty of all save herself and the staff. Parsons, with time to spare, led Sarah from one room to the next, throwing open doors to empty rooms, dressing-rooms and bathrooms.

'I'll never find my way round,' worried Sarah.

'Yes, you will, and anyway you only come up here with me in the evenings for the beds—that's when there are guests. You'll do the rooms each morning, of course, but Mrs Legge will have told you about that.'

After the bedrooms, Sarah was taken downstairs and shown where the cleaning things were housed. 'And everything has to be put back clean and tidy. Now, I'm off to help in the dining-room—you go and lay the table for our supper and get the early morning tea-trays ready.'

Supper was a sustaining meal: steak and kidney pie, and rice pudding for afters, and Mrs Legge graciously allowed Sarah to take some of the pudding with her for Charles. 'And you'd better get to your bed,' she said, not unkindly. 'Got an alarm, have you? Half-past six, then, and I'll want you here in the kitchen to give Cook a hand by seven o'clock. You can have twenty minutes to make your bed and tidy your room after our breakfast at eight o'clock. Do your work well and I'll not object if you pop over to see that cat of yours once in a while.'

Sarah thanked her and, bearing the milk pudding, went across the yard to her room. Charles was pleased to see her, ate the pudding with pleasure and accompanied her into the yard. It was a pleasant evening, and the air was fresh after the streets of London. She bore Charles back indoors, undressed and showered rapidly and curled up on the divan with him beside her. The list of her duties was a long one and she went over it anxiously in her mind, but it wouldn't all be work—she was to have a half-day each Wednesday and a day off on

Sundays, and every afternoon she was free from
two o'clock until four. She would manage, she told
Charles sleepily as she closed her eyes. But strangely
enough her last waking thoughts weren't of any of
these things—she wondered what the Professor was
doing.

He was at his elegant Knightsbridge house, sitting
in his study behind his desk strewn with the various
letters and forms he should have been dealing with
and wasn't. His austere good looks were marred by
the splendid rage he had kept bottled up all day
and now, in the peace and quiet of his own home,
he gave vent to it.

He had returned to London on the previous day
and had gone, as was his wont, to his outpatients
clinic in the morning. It wasn't until he had opened
the door opposite Sarah's desk that he'd admitted
to himself that, although he had no interest in the
girl whatsoever, it would be interesting to see her
again. Only, the desk had been empty and so had
been the chair behind it.

He'd wished Mrs Pearce and Mrs Drew good
morning, and had then said, 'Miss Fletcher? Is she
ill?'

'Made redundant,' Mrs Drew said; 'Sacked,' Mrs
Pearce had said rather more loudly.

'Indeed. May I ask why?'

'She was three days late coming back from her
leave, sir,' Mrs Pearce had said—she didn't stand
in such awe of him as Mrs Drew. 'She did the same
thing last year, and Miss Payne told her then she'd
have to alter her ways. Miss Payne didn't much like
her, and when she asked why Sarah—Miss Fletcher,

that is—hadn't come back when she said she would, she said she'd written and asked if she might stay another few days. But the letter never got here— there was a strike—she and Miss Payne had words, and Miss Payne got her sacked.'

The Professor's face could have been carved in stone and he'd said nothing at all, although both ladies had leaned back a little in their chairs just as though he had been hurling abuse at them. 'And where has Miss Fletcher gone now?' he'd asked, his voice carefully impersonal.

Mrs Pearce had shaken her head. 'No idea, sir. Got another job, I dare say, though Miss Payne gave her a reference that wouldn't have helped her much.'

The Professor had thanked her gravely and gone along to his room where his registrar had been waiting for him. He was an astute young man, who'd taken one look at his chief's eyes, as grey as winter water, and forborne to ask him whether he had had a successful series of lectures.

They had both become immersed in the morning's work and it wasn't until lunchtime, his clinic over, that the Professor had gone to Miss Payne's office. He had been there for ten minutes or so and Miss Payne, very much shaken, had had to be buoyed up with cups of strong tea after he had gone.

That evening, after an interminable afternoon, he had driven himself to Sarah's lodgings, summoned Mrs Potter from her basement and requested information about Sarah. 'She is still here?' he'd asked.

'Lor' bless you, no, sir. Out of work she was for a couple of weeks, then comes back one day and packs her bags and takes the cat and off she goes. Got a job—didn't say where—a long way orf, she told me. Left a small trunk of 'er bits and pieces in me box-room, said someone'd fetch 'em.'

'How long has she been gone?'

'Yesterday. Didn't leave no forwarding address. Never 'ad no letters ter send on.'

He had thanked her politely and given her money. 'If you should hear from Miss Fletcher, would you telephone this number?' He had scribbled in his notebook and then torn out the page.

Mrs Potter had fingered the money in her hand. 'That I will, sir. Likely she'll let me know that she will be coming for the trunk.'

He had bidden her goodnight with cold courtesy and gone home, ate the delicious dinner his cook had prepared for him with an indifference which cut her to the quick, and shut himself in his study. He had no interest in the wretched girl, of course; on the other hand he felt quite responsible for her dismissal, unjustified though it was. He cast his powerful mind back upon events and remembered that he had urged her to say nothing about her visit to his home—a request which she had obeyed to the letter, with disastrous consequences for herself. He would have to find her. He sighed heavily and stretched out a hand for the phone.

His mother, suppressing maternal curiosity, was unable to recall any clue which might lead to Sarah's plans. 'I know she had a stepmother who more or less turned her out of the house after her father died. A pity Fletcher is such a common name—I

mean, one wouldn't know where to begin to look...
Surely her landlady has some idea?'

She listened to the Professor's testy explanation
and said, 'Well, dear, if you will hang on for a few
minutes I'll ask everyone here.'

She put down the receiver and turned to her
husband, explaining quickly. 'And if you are asking
me,' she added, 'he's interested in Sarah . . .'

Mijnheer Nauta looked up from the book he was
reading. 'That little thing? Nice girl, but not his
type, my dear. It's natural he should be concerned
about someone who worked for him.'

He went back to his book and his wife hurried
off to the kitchen to ask everyone there if Sarah
had mentioned at any time where she had lived
before she had gone to London to work.

She had no luck, although there was a good deal
of concern expressed, for they had all liked her.
She picked up the phone again to tell the Professor
that she had drawn a blank. He thanked her, but
he didn't waste time in discussing what was to be
done next. He bade her goodnight and hung up.

The next day he went back to Sarah's lodgings,
but this time he didn't summon Mrs Potter. He went
up the stairs and knocked on the first of three doors
on the first landing. Its occupant was home and
invited him in, but in answer to his questions shook
her head. 'Very quiet, was Sarah,' he was told.
'Never talked about herself, kept herself to herself,
too. Not snooty, just shy, and if you'll wait a minute
I'll get the other girls.'

There were three more girls living in the house,
none of whom knew anything about Sarah, although they all conceded that she was a nice girl

and always willing to lend tea and milk and take messages.

The Professor thanked them and left the house, calling in at the off-licence at the corner of the street and arranging for a couple of bottles of sherry to be sent round that evening. He scribbled a note with the reminder that he could be reached at the phone number he wrote down.

The need to find her became an obsession but only, he reminded himself, because he felt responsible for her misfortune. The hospital authorities had been unable to help—the only address they had ever had was that of Sarah's bedsitter. They kindly looked up her records for him, disclosing the fact that she had had six months at a secretarial school, and that although her typing was adequate she had failed lamentably in shorthand. A good all-round worker, he was told, well educated and with a pleasant manner towards the patients.

'I'm surprised you allowed her to leave,' observed the Professor drily.

Authority looked as offended as it dared. 'Hospital rules must be observed, Professor Nauta, and Miss Fletcher broke a most important rule on two consecutive occasions.'

The Professor rumbled a terse answer and left.

'Devil take the girl,' he declared fiercely as he stalked across the forecourt to his car. 'I'll find her if it's the last thing I do—and give her a piece of my mind when I do.' He got into his car, still muttering darkly, this time in Dutch.

The next few days were unprofitable, so that his temper remained uncertain, and Brindle, who with his wife the cook ran the Professor's house so admirably for him, went around tut-tutting at his master's gloom. It was pure chance that, towards the end of the week, offered a clue. One of the girls staying in a room at Mrs Potter's, sipping the excellent sherry which the Professor had sent round, remembered that Sarah had once made a vague reference to a boutique in Tunbridge Wells. 'I dare say it's a wild-goose chase,' she said over the phone, 'but we were talking about clothes, and she mentioned that she had bought something at this shop... you could try.'

The Professor thanked her warmly, arranged for more sherry to be delivered and at the weekend drove himself to Tunbridge Wells, where he tracked down the boutique and without hesitation went inside.

The saleslady eyed him with some doubt—he didn't look like a husband or a boyfriend searching for something for his wife or girlfriend.

The Professor, a truthful man, had his story ready, and she answered happily enough. Indeed, Miss Fletcher had been a good customer although Mrs Fletcher, who still came to the shop, had told her that she had gone to live in London and had a marvellous job. She gave him Mrs Fletcher's address readily enough, and only then remembered to ask who he was.

'A family friend?' she ventured. 'Miss Fletcher is well, I hope? Such a nice young lady.'

'Her doctor,' said the Professor at his most bland. 'Friends of hers abroad have asked me to look her up. I've not seen her myself for some time, and I was told in London that she would possibly be at home. But no one was sure of her address, although they remembered you.'

He thanked her politely and made his escape—his story was thin and full of holes, which presently the saleslady, if she had the leisure, would discover for herself. He got back into his car and drove himself to the village whose name he had been given, and turned the car into a well-kept drive, stopping before the door of a small manor house.

He took his time about ringing the bell while he looked around. The house, now that he came to think about it, was exactly the kind of place in which Sarah might have spent her youth. He didn't know her well—indeed, he reminded himself, he didn't wish to—but she wasn't a town girl.

He rang the bell and a pert maid took his name and admitted him, showed him into a long, low room with panelled walls and a beautiful plaster ceiling, and went to fetch her mistress. Which gave him time to perfect his tale. A pack of lies, he told himself savagely, the girl had been nothing but a nuisance...

Mrs Fletcher was tall, a well-preserved forty and handsomely dressed. She listened to the Professor's reasons for his visit—this time he was calling on behalf of an old friend of Sarah's who had lost touch while he was out of the country... 'I said that, as I was coming this way for the weekend, I would call at her home and let him know if she was here.'

Mrs Fletcher said carelessly, 'Oh, she had any number of friends while she lived here. Most of them have gone away and several are married. It is some years since she was here. You know her?'

The Professor looked her in the eye. 'No, not at all,' he assured her. Which was the truth, he told himself silently; he might have met her, watched her play the piano half the night, wished her good day on his way to and from his clinic, but he still didn't know her...

'Well, I haven't the least idea where she is,' said her stepmother. 'After all, she's twenty-eight and leads her own life.'

The Professor sipped the tea she had offered him. 'I was under the impression that she lived here,' he said casually. 'This is a charming house. I envy you the peace and quiet.'

She rolled her eyes at him and looked arch. 'It can be boring. I come up to town quite often. Perhaps we could meet...'

'A delightful idea, Mrs Fletcher.' She saw him smile at her quite charmingly. 'Much though I regret it, I really must go. I have promised to be in Winchelsea by early evening.'

He got back into his car and drove away, back to his home, frowning at the idea of Sarah having to live with someone like Mrs Fletcher. She hadn't lived with her, of course—she had gone to London, and become one of thousands of other girls earning their livings in the anonymity of a big city.

During the next few days, he told himself several times that there was no point in continuing his search. As her stepmother had pointed out, Sarah was no young girl. By now she would have found herself another job, far better paid, probably, and settled herself into a new home. He winced at the word 'home'—bedsitters weren't home, however hard one tried to make them so. He had little enough leisure that week, but what time he had he spent in his search for Sarah. Roundabout enquiries brought no results.

The Professor refused to admit that he was wasting his time. All the same, he took the daughter of an old friend out to dinner one evening and did his best to be interested in her, and when his godmother invited him to spend the weekend with her, he accepted. He had been working hard, and a couple of days out of London would be pleasant. Early on Saturday morning he got into his car and drove himself away, to the relief of his devoted staff who had had to put up with his ill temper for some time now.

He arrived mid-morning, and Cork opened the door to him with a welcoming smile. 'Lady Wesley is in the drawing-room, sir,' he said in dignified tones, and the Professor went past him into the hall.

The first person he saw was Sarah, very neat in her housemaid's uniform, trotting briskly towards the dining-room with a tray of silver ready for Parsons to lay the table.

CHAPTER FOUR

THE Professor had crossed the hall and was blocking Sarah's way before she could do more than gasp.

'Damn it, girl, what the devil are you doing here?' He spoke quite softly but she took a step backwards, hugging her tray, for he looked ferocious.

She said, in a voice which shook only a very little, 'You should mind your language, Professor. And, as you very well see, I am the housemaid here.'

She saw Cork treading majestically towards them, but the Professor had seen him too and waved him away, so she went on, 'If you don't go away, you will get me dismissed—and that will be twice.' She added, 'It's no good looking so ill-tempered. Parsons is waiting for this tray.'

Parsons had come to the dining-room door to see what was happening. The Professor beckoned her over, took the tray from Sarah, gave it to her with a smile and turned his attention to Sarah.

'You are behaving very badly, Professor,' said Sarah severely. 'I must ask you to go away——'

'I've just arrived for the weekend.' His voice was silky. 'So I was the reason for getting you dismissed from St Cyprian's?'

'You weren't there to explain, and you asked me not to tell anyone——'

He enquired coldly, 'And did you not wonder why I requested you to be silent about your stay in Holland?'

'Well, of course I wondered, but I didn't worry about it.' She cast an anxious eye at Cork, who had stationed himself at the back of the hall.

'Have you never heard of the hospital grapevine?'

She smiled widely, humouring him. 'Of course— it's a red-hot pipeline of gossip and scandal. You have no idea——' She stopped, staring up at him. 'Oh, dear...'

'Exactly, Miss Fletcher. I'm glad to see that your wits haven't entirely deserted you. How old are you?'

'That's none of your business.' Her voice was tart. 'I'm twenty-eight.'

'By now you should have absorbed at least some of the pitfalls of modern society, but it seems you are still walking around with your head in a paper bag.'

'Of all the rude men!' she burst out. 'You're making me out to be a freak.'

He said smoothly, 'No freak, Miss Fletcher—you are that rarity: a very nice, well-brought-up girl.'

He gave her a smile as cold as his eyes, and crossed the hall to where Cork was standing. 'Lady Wesley is expecting me?' he asked pleasantly, and went into the drawing-room.

Cork trod majestically to where Sarah was standing. That he disapproved of servants, especially a housemaid, passing the time of day with guests went without saying. On the other hand, Sarah wasn't the usual type of servant—that they had all agreed upon in the kitchen. Not in the least

toffee-nosed, but definitely from the other side of
the baize-door... He said now, eyeing her
woebegone face, 'Now, now, Sarah, don't take on
so. No harm done. Gentlemen have their little
flashes of temper, you know, and he was took by
surprise. Known 'im long, 'ave you?'

She shook her head. 'No, Mr Cork, I was just a
clerk at the hospital where he is a consultant. I'm
sorry if you are annoyed. I wouldn't have spoken
to him if he hadn't recognised me.'

'We'll forget about it. Now get on with your
work, there's a good girl.'

The Professor greeted his godmother, enquired after
her health, gave her news of his family in Holland,
remarked on the weather, and over a cup of coffee
observed, 'Your new housemaid, Aunt Beatrice.'

'Such a nice girl,' declared Lady Wesley. 'Not at
all what one would expect, and such a splendid
worker. Even Cork is satisfied with her, and that
is praise indeed. So willing, too, running here and
there and everywhere for Cook, who as you know
has trouble with her feet now. I'm thankful that
she is so well-liked in the kitchen. She has a cat,
called Charles. Cork tells me that he is no trouble
to anyone.' She frowned. 'I feel that perhaps I
should try to discover why she is in domestic service.
It is so obvious that she comes from a good background, although she has never given a hint of it.
Mrs Legge tells me that she can turn out a room
twice as quickly and thoroughly as any housemaid
she has ever had working for her.'

'A paragon,' observed the Professor drily.

'And an honest one. She told me that she had been dismissed from her job in a hospital because she was late back from her holidays. She made no excuses, just sat there waiting to hear what I would have to say about that. Couldn't find any clerical work, so sensibly looked for work where it was to be had.' She eyed her godson shrewdly. 'Why are you so interested in her, Radolf?'

'The hospital where she worked is St Cyprian's, and I, most regrettably, am the cause of her getting dismissed.'

'Get her reinstated.'

'Easily done, but I suspect that she wouldn't thank me for that. The head of her department has taken a dislike to her—life would be made miserable for her.'

'Did she have a flat or somewhere to live?'

'A bedsitter, with a balcony—for Charles the cat.'

Lady Wesley was careful to keep her voice disinterested. She had long ago given up all hope of Radolf's marrying—surely he wasn't seriously interested in the rather plain girl who was her housemaid?

As though he had read her thoughts, he said shortly, 'I feel responsible.'

'Yes, dear, but is it fair of you to try and arrange her life for her? I am aware that she should be sitting here with us instead of making beds and polishing the furniture; I am also aware that she is at least in her own environment. Do you suppose that she was happy in this bedsitter of hers? And did she like living in London?'

The Professor frowned. 'I have not had the occasion to ask her.'

His godmother took him up briskly. 'Well, of course not—stupid of me—anyway, you can see for yourself that she has a job and somewhere to live, and I imagine that she is a good deal happier here than she was in London.'

'But she isn't a servant——'

'She is my housemaid, Radolf, and if she is satisfied with her work here, I hardly think that you need to concern yourself with her. Was she pleased to see you?'

He examined the nails of his well-kept hands. 'No.'

'In that case, dear boy, leave well alone. I'm sure you are relieved now that you know where she is and that she isn't in want. Now do come out into the garden and look at my very early roses—they are going to give a splendid display this year.'

He saw little more of Sarah that weekend: a glimpse of piled-up hair under a neat cap, a distant view of a starched cotton dress disappearing round a corner, the murmur of her voice as she trotted to and fro fetching and carrying for Parsons or Cork. And she for her part avoided him, and explained in her nice, quiet voice to the assembled staff at the dinner table how she and Professor Nauta happened to have met. She told them the truth, too, only cutting out the bits which she thought might annoy him if she was to tell them. Cork had given it as his opinion that the incident in the hall, regrettable though it was, was hardly her fault and pronounced forgiveness, seconded by Mrs Legge with a background chorus of agreement by everyone else. Sarah wasn't quite one of them, they had decided among themselves, but she was a very nice girl, gentle and quiet and always willing. She wasn't stuck-up either, and she knew her place.

It was a week later that Cork informed the staff that the household would be transferring to London for a month. 'This is Lady Wesley's habit each year,' he explained pompously to Sarah. 'She has a town house just off Grosvenor Square, and with the exception of Mrs Legge and Molly, who remain here to caretake, and the gardener, who remains also, we staff her London establishment. We travel up the day before so that everything is in readiness when she arrives. There is a housekeeper in residence and a kitchen maid, so that there is not a great deal to be done when we arrive there. Mrs Butler the housekeeper will see you all and arrange your free times. You will come to me if you have any problems.'

Sarah waited until Cork was at his most benign, after supper as he sat in his special chair with his evening glass of beer.

'I'm rather worried about Charles, Mr Cork,' she began. 'I suppose it wouldn't be possible for Molly to go to London in my place, and allow me to stay here and do her work?'

For all his pomposity he was a kind man, and he liked her. 'Well, now, Sarah, I think that very unlikely. Molly is a good girl, but not versed in the ways of the gentry—a bit rough and ready, as you might say. I cannot allow you to alter your position, Sarah, but the staff-rooms at the London house are adequate, and two or three of them are on the basement level with windows opening on to quite a nice garden. I will see that you have one of these rooms so that Charles may have access to the garden.'

Sarah thanked him, wished him goodnight and went to her little cottage to explain to Charles. 'And I'm so afraid that I shall see Professor Nauta again,' she finished, 'but it is only for a month and St Cyprian's is miles away from Grosvenor Square.'

Charles, gobbling up his supper, had no interest in the matter.

The next few days were busy—the house had to be left in apple-pie order, and at the same time there was a good deal of packing-up to do. They left early in the morning, with Knott driving the big station-wagon; he would deposit them at the London house and return to fetch Lady Wesley and Mudd, her personal maid, this time driving the Jaguar.

There was little time for Sarah to do more than admire the pristine face of the house, one of many in a terrace in a quiet street. Once inside, via the tradesman's entrance, she was kept busy finding her way around, conscious that Mrs Butler's deceptively mild eyes were here, there and everywhere. By the time Lady Wesley arrived, the house bore the appearance of a smoothly run household with flowers in the rooms, beds freshly made and a tantalising whiff of something cooking in the basement kitchen every time the baize door at the back of the hall was opened.

Something which Lady Wesley took for granted, although she praised Mrs Butler in a vague way when she arrived. 'It all looks very nice, Mrs Butler. How beautifully you run the house,' she had observed; it never entered her head that her staff had been toiling for hours to achieve the perfection she expected. She went to the elegant drawing-room and asked for tea to be brought, just as her domestic staff were gathering for half an hour's peace round their own teapot, and it was Sarah who took it to her. It should have been Mr Cork, but he had gone to his room to have a nap and Parsons had taken off her shoes and couldn't get them on again.

'Where is Cork?' Lady Wesley wanted to know.

'In the cellar, my lady,' said Sarah, improvising rapidly, 'checking the wines.' And, before Lady Wesley could say anything, 'Parsons has gone to check the linen cupboard with Mrs Butler.'

Lady Wesley smiled, pleased to hear of everyone's industry. 'You may put the tray here on this table, Fletcher. And tell Cook that I should like dinner put forward half an hour.'

Cook grumbled and heaved herself to her feet. 'So I'd best get on with that sauce.'

Mrs Butler, refilling Sarah's cooling tea, said, 'Sarah, give Parsons a hand with the table and then come back here and lay our supper.' She nodded towards the other girl there, the kitchen maid. 'Kitty, start on the pans and get our tea things washed up.'

Sarah trotted to and fro, thinking longingly of her bed and Charles' cosy company. True to his promise, Cork had given her a room at the back of the house and, although she hadn't dared to let Charles out, there was a wide window-sill where he could sit and watch the garden. He had been fed and his bed, a cardboard box lined with a piece of blanket Parsons had found her, was beside the divan, but he would be glad to see her.

The evening wore on and finally, after the generous supper Mrs Butler supplied, she was free to go to her room. She undressed rapidly, went along the passage to the bathroom she shared with Parsons and Cook, and then climbed thankfully into bed. The room wasn't as pleasant as the one at Lady Wesley's country house, but the view was quite nice from the window. Besides, she assured herself as she dropped off, Charles heavy in the crook of her arm, it was only for a month. She spared a thought for the Professor as she closed her eyes, a habit she had got into without quite knowing why.

She was awake by six o'clock and, mindful of Charles' needs, wormed her person through the old-fashioned sash-window, and with him walking cautiously beside her, wandered through the high-walled garden—too high for him to climb, she saw thankfully. He went back willingly enough into her room presently, accepted his breakfast and curled up for another nap, leaving her free to finish dressing and go upstairs to the front hall to draw curtains in the big rooms and open the windows, before departing to the kitchen for the cup of tea which awaited her.

No one else was up yet, only herself and the kitchen maid. She laid tea-trays, set the table in the servants' hall for breakfast and collected everything Parsons would need for setting lunch in the dining-room. Lady Wesley had guests for that meal, and Parsons would have plenty to do before they arrived. Kitty was getting everything ready for Cook, and after a while took tea to Mrs Butler and Cook. Cork made his own tea in his room and appeared shortly, ready to cast his eye over things. By now Sarah had hoovered and dusted the dining-room and was busy in the drawing-room. She paused long enough to wish him a cheerful good morning, and then began the delicate task of dusting. Breakfast was a cheerful meal, but by suppertime they all admitted that the London house presented far more hard work than the country home. On the other hand, as Parsons said, there were the delights of the London shops and enter-tainments to compensate for that.

Within the week they agreed among themselves that shops and cinemas were all very well, but they hardly compensated for the long hours and extra work. Lady Wesley was living it up in a majestic sort of way and it was Miss Mudd who suffered most, for her ladyship dined out a good deal, visited the theatre followed by supper parties, and in her turn gave large dinner parties in her own house. Which meant that the silver had to be cleaned, glasses polished until they sparkled and there was an almost endless round of preparing meals and clearing them away. Mrs Butler brooked no skimping.

The weather had turned warm, and it seemed as though summer was about to burst upon them with unexpected sun and blue skies. The nicest time of the day from Sarah's point of view was very early in the morning, when she and Charles wandered round the garden beyond her room with the sleeping house, the curtains drawn over its windows, at their backs.

It was during the second week that Sarah came, so to speak, face to face with the Professor once more. Lady Wesley was going to the theatre and, making her stately way down the stairs, had in some inexplicable way dropped one of her rings. Mudd, ordered to find it immediately and at a great disadvantage since she had left her glasses in the kitchen, floundered around in a despairing way until Lady Wesley ordered her to fetch someone to help her. Sarah happened to be the first person Miss Mudd saw as she scuttled down to the kitchen, and she obediently followed her to the hall and stairs.

At first glance there was no sign of any ring. Sarah went to the top of the staircase and began painstakingly to crawl backwards, searching every tread. She was halfway down when the front doorbell rang and Cork trod silently to open it, giving the Professor an enticing view of Sarah's small person back to front. He paused to take a second look, and at the same time she cried triumphantly, 'Here it is, Lady Wesley,' and looked over her shoulder.

The Professor was looking his best: a dinner-jacket, exquisitely tailored, set off his formidable proportions to perfection, his snowy shirt-front was severely plain and dazzlingly white, his shoes gleamed—a sight to delight any girl, although his appearance seemed to have the opposite effect upon Sarah, who got to her feet with great dignity, her face red, and, ignoring him, handed the ring to Lady Wesley and enquired in exactly the right tone of voice if that would be all.

Lady Wesley took the ring and thanked her pleasantly, adding, 'Now you have to get back to your work, Fletcher.' At the same time she noticed the frown on her godson's face and gave an inward chuckle. The girl had got under his hitherto impervious skin, she decided. She greeted him with warmth, remarking, 'Such a sensible girl, if she stays on long enough I shall get Mudd to train her as a lady's maid—she can take over when Mudd retires.'

She wasn't sure, but she thought that she heard the Professor grind his teeth.

'Have we time for a drink before we go?' she asked. 'Come into the drawing-room, my dear. Have you had a busy day? Well, this evening should be pleasant. That delightful Grace Kingsley is joining us, you know. So pretty, and she dresses so well.'

The Professor poured their drinks and made some non-committal remark. He didn't care two straws for Grace, a pretty girl if you liked blue-eyed blondes with rather shrill voices and a complete lack of intelligence. He handed Lady Wesley her drink and sat down opposite her.

'Having a good time?' he asked her.

'Oh, delightful, Radolf. And so different from my life in the country. I seldom go to bed before one o'clock, and sometimes two is striking. It's a little hard on Mudd, who isn't as young as she was. I think I shall ask Fletcher to wait up for me in the future—she's young and strong... I dare say Mrs Butler can let her have an hour or so off in the afternoon to make up.'

The Professor appeared uninterested. 'Why not get another maid?' he asked lazily.

'Oh, the staff wouldn't like that. Besides, they like Sarah, they'll see that she gets her free time.'

'And when is that at the moment?'

Lady Wesley looked doubtful. 'Well, now I come to think of it, it is each afternoon. Oh, well, I shall think of something. In any case, she has every Sunday free.'

Without a spark of interest, the Professor observed, 'Oh, yes?' He put down his glass. 'Should we be going?' He smiled at her. 'You look very splendid tonight, my dear.'

She said complacently, 'Yes, I know I do, Radolf,' and sailed ahead of him, not in the least deceived by his lack of interest in her housemaid, to where Cork was waiting to open the door for them.

The play was excellent; the Professor sat through it, saying all the right things to the charming Grace, apparently absorbed in what was going on on the stage, bottling up the ill temper which the sight of Sarah engendered in him. A thoroughly tiresome girl, he told himself, bending a deaf ear to Grace's vapid chatter, who contrived without saying a single word to make him feel guilty. And why she had to go off in that ridiculous fashion and get a job as a domestic was something he would never understand. She had only to apply to him and he would have got her reinstated, even done his best to find her more suitable lodgings. The very least she could have done would have been to let him know that she had left St Cyprian's. Was she aware that he had spent a good deal of his leisure looking for her? By the end of the performance he was in a towering rage, all the worse for having to conceal it. He sat through supper at the fashionable restaurant Lady Wesley had chosen, his bland good manners masking his feelings. But, once he had taken her back home and driven himself back to his own house, he repaired to his study, dismissed the faithful Brindle, and immersed himself in his work, recording replies to his letters ready for his secretary to type in the morning.

His rage had worn itself out by the time he had finished, and he sat back in his chair, ruefully admitting that Sarah had done exactly what he would have expected her to do. She was a proud piece, but he liked her for that. She also annoyed him excessively and he knew why, although he wasn't going to admit it even to himself. He put a hand down to stroke the head of the Golden Labrador sitting patiently beside him. 'We'll go to bed, Trotter, and I promise you that I'll not waste any more time over the girl. She is quite capable of looking after herself.'

A remark which set the Olympian gods chuckling.

Sundays were oases in the weekly desert of hard work for Sarah. She spent them roaming the parks, feeding the ducks with the stale bread Cook had given her, eating sparingly herself from one of the stalls to be found. Come teatime, she took herself back to her room, fed Charles, made herself tea on her gas ring, ate the buns she'd brought back with her and then, after a brief sojourn in the back garden, she dressed herself neatly and took herself off to church. She enjoyed evensong and, over and above that, it was impossible to feel lonely in church.

On this, the third Sunday of their stay in London, she had lingered rather longer than usual in Green

Park and so had taken a short-cut to reach the church before the service started. The streets were quiet, with few people about. She turned into the narrow road which would bring her out in front of All Saints Church, and became aware that halfway down there were three people behaving rather strangely. Youths, circling around a fourth figure who was walking resolutely ahead as though they weren't there. She hurried a little, not yet frightened but apprehensive. She was quite close when all the youths made a concerted rush at the elderly man, who turned to face them.

Sarah unslung her shoulder-bag, heavy with hymn and prayer books, and aimed it at the youth ahead of her. It caught him behind the knees so that he toppled over and, much heartened by this success, she swung the bag once more towards a second youth. Her aim wasn't so good this time— it caught him on the shoulder, and although it stopped him for a moment he regained his balance almost at once and, leaving his companion to deal with the man, turned on her.

The Professor, on his way home from an emergency call at the hospital, had taken a short-cut too. He pulled up, jumped out and prepared to do battle just as Sarah was given a vicious thump which laid her out on the pavement with a quite sickening crash. He stepped over the youth she had felled with her shoulder-bag, caught the boy's two companions by their jacket collars, shook them so that their teeth rattled, pitched them on to their knees and begged them in tones of cold rage to stay just where they were before turning his attention to the elderly man bending over Sarah. It was someone he knew: Sir William Pettigrew, a highly esteemed consultant at St Cyprian's, now retired.

'Sir William, you're not hurt?'

His eye fell upon Sarah, lying in an untidy heap on the pavement, and he got down on his knees beside her. 'I might have known it,' he said bitterly. 'Only you could disturb the peace of a Sunday for me. Why in the name of all that's holy must you get involved——?'

Sarah opened one eye. 'You're very rude. Go away, do.'

Sir William had listened in some surprise to this. 'My dear Radolph! This brave young lady came to my aid—indeed, she wielded her handbag in a masterly fashion. She has taken a nasty tumble, too.' He glanced uneasily at the three youths. 'What should we do?'

'There's a phone in my car, sir,' said the Professor. 'Dial for the police, if you would, while I see if Sarah is hurt.'

Sir William did as he was bid, and came back to hover over Sarah. 'You know each other?' he asked, watching the Professor's large hands gently exploring Sarah's head.

'All this hair,' he muttered crossly, and took out the pins. 'Unfortunately, yes,' he said.

Sarah opened an eye once more. She had a headache, but she still had her wits. She said clearly, 'We dislike each other. It is my earnest wish that I never see the man again. He has no feelings and, if he has, they're deep-frozen.'

And then, despite the headache, she fell into a refreshing sleep.

The police arrived in a patrol car, took brief statements from Sir William and the Professor, who had lifted Sarah into his car and was cleaning up a small cut on the top of her head, and removed the youths.

'If you could come down to the station in the morning, sir?' they wanted to know. 'The young lady needs a bit of care, I dare say. When she's fit enough we'd like a word with her, too.'

The Professor nodded. 'Nothing serious, I think. You can contact both Sir William and me through St Cyprian's. Miss Fletcher will have to be warded for a couple of days. If you would ring and enquire in the morning?'

The police went, Sir William climbed into the back of the Professor's car and he turned it round and drove back to the hospital.

Sir William wanted to go home. 'If I might suggest,' said the Professor, 'it would be a good idea if someone just looked you over—you had a few knocks?'

'Well, yes. I would have been stunned, I fancy, if this darling child hadn't rushed to help me. A veritable virago...'

'You can say that again,' murmured the Professor.

Sir William thrust his elderly face over the seat to look at her. She was lolling beside the Professor, her eyes closed. She opened them and said urgently, 'Charles...'

'Her boyfriend,' declared Sir William, who was sentimental.

'Her cat,' said the Professor, who was not. 'Can you understand me, Sarah? I'll take care of him.

I'm taking you to St Cyprian's, and you'll have to stay the night.' She made a small protesting sound and he said impatiently, 'Don't fuss.'

'If this is your bedside manner,' muttered Sarah, who felt peculiar and wasn't quite sure what she was talking about, 'I am surprised that you can make a living.' She dozed off again and didn't hear his rumble of laughter.

The next morning she had only the vaguest recollection of being examined in Casualty, X-rayed and then warded. She was in a pleasant room by herself, she noted with surprise, and when a nurse came presently to take her temperature and ask her how she felt, she wanted to know why she wasn't in a main ward.

The nurse looked surprised. 'Why, Professor Nauta said that you were to come here to PP. You're to stay in bed until he sees you this morning. I say, is it true you routed several muggers who attacked Sir William Pettigrew?'

Sarah shook her head and winced because the headache, though faint, was still there. 'I managed to knock one over with my shoulder-bag, but I missed the second one and he knocked me down, so really I wasn't much good.'

The nurse smiled. 'Well, Sir William was full of your courage. You used to work in the clinics, didn't you. I dare say they'll offer you your job back.'

'I've got a good job.'

'Lucky you. I'm going to bring you a cup of tea and then some breakfast. Do you fancy anything special?'

A bang on the head had its compensations, thought Sarah. 'Could I have some buttered toast?'

There was never time to make toast in the servants' hall.

The Professor came just before noon, flanked by his registrar and Sister Black, who had ruled over PP for a decade or more. He bade Sarah good morning, assured her that there was nothing abnormal in the X-rays, asked her if her head ached, prescribed tablets and told her that she might go back to her own room on the following day. 'Light duties only,' he told her. 'I've already spoken to your employer. Tomorrow morning the police wish to take a statement from you. You may return to your room after tea.' He gave her a steely look. 'Good day to you, Miss Fletcher.'

Beyond yes or no, Sarah had said nothing. Now she said quite sharply, 'Just a moment, Professor Nauta,' and, when he turned in surprise, 'Thank you for bringing me here—I'm grateful.'

To which he made no answer, his eyes cold. They stared at each other for a moment before he went away.

Ten minutes later Sister Black came in. 'Professor Nauta asked me to tell you that Charles is quite all right, and being well looked after.'

Sarah felt a desire to burst into tears; she had been longing to ask the Professor about her cat, but in the face of his cold, impersonal manner she hadn't been able to utter a word. She said, 'Oh, Sister, thank you for telling me—he's my cat...' She found that she was crying, great gulping sobs which she couldn't control any more, and after a moment Sister Black sat down on the bed and put an arm round her while Sarah wept all over her pristine uniform.

'There, there,' said Sister Black. 'There's nothing like a good cry to relieve the feelings. Now, everything is all right, you're to stay in bed today and I shall send a nurse in with a nice tray of tea and one of the tablets Professor Nauta has written up for you. You'll have a nice nap directly after lunch.'

She gave Sarah a comforting pat on the shoulder and sailed away and presently, much heartened by the tea, Sarah sat up and ate the light lunch she was given. Then, obedient to Sister Black's instructions, she had a nice nap.

When she woke there was a delightful floral arrangement on her bedside table: roses and carnations and freesias in a charming little basket. Sarah sat up and opened the envelope propped up beside it. It read, 'With grateful thanks and compliments from Sir William Pettigrew.'

Sarah sniffed at its fragrance and told herself how silly she had been imagining, even for a moment, that the flowers were from the Professor.

His registrar came to see her the next day, pronounced her fit and well and told her that she might go back to her room. So she dressed, had her tea, wished Sister Black and the nurses goodbye and took herself down to the hospital entrance. Sister had said that there would be transport for her and she looked around for an ambulance, one of those which took outpatients to and fro each day. There wasn't one in sight, but Knott was there with the car. He came to her as soon as he saw her, looking very pleased to see her.

'Well, that was a pretty kettle of fish and no mistake,' he observed, helping her into the car. 'We've all been that anxious . . .'

She turned a surprised face to him. 'Were you? Really? How kind of you, it was silly to fall over like that.'

'If I'd have been there I'd have belted the three of them. Knocking young ladies about, a lot of young thugs. A good thing Professor Nauta came along when he did and gave them what for.' He gave her an anxious glance. 'You're OK again?'

'I feel fine, thank you, Mr Knott. I hope no one minded doing my work, I'm sorry——'

'Proud to do it, Sarah. Here we are, you're to go straight to Mrs Butler.'

But she was waylaid on the way there by Parsons and Miss Mudd and Cork, all wanting to know if she was all right—even Miss Mudd expressed ladylike concern. Rather overwhelmed by their kindness, Sarah presented herself before Mrs Butler and was surprised once more by being told to sit down.

'We are all proud of you,' Mrs Butler told her. 'It's no easy thing to face up to these bullies. Now, Professor Nauta has been to see Lady Wesley and came to see me at the same time. You are to take things very easily for a few days. No work before breakfast, a rest in the afternoon and you are to go to bed directly supper is finished. You may do a little light housework and help ready the bedrooms in the evening, but that is all. If you feel quite yourself by the end of the week, that will be splendid, and I am to let him know and he will decide if you are fit for your full duties.' She smiled a little. 'You will find that Charles is quite happy— we have all been looking after him. Now, go to your room and come over for your supper presently.'

Charles was delighted to see her, and someone had put some flowers in a vase by the dressing-table and Knott had arranged the basket of flowers from Sir William on the window-sill. Sarah heaved a sigh of content—it could have been so much worse. She might have broken an arm or a leg and been out of work once more, and everyone had been so kind. A kind girl herself, she was always surprised and pleased when people were kind to her.

At supper Parsons pointed out that the skirt she was wearing had been badly torn when she fell. 'You ought to get yourself something new,' she advised.

'Well, I'd like to,' said Sarah, faintly peevish, 'but the shops don't open on Sundays.'

Mrs Butler looked up from her plate. 'In that case, Sarah, you shall have your next day off during the week.' She paused to think. 'Thursday will suit me very well.'

By Thursday, Sarah felt quite herself again. With her wages in her purse and a neat list of things she intended to buy, she set off for Oxford Street. First, she had decided, she would take a good look in the shop windows and then embark on her purchases, but when she got to Oxford Circus she turned into Regent Street. A quick look at the up-market shops, she promised herself, before going to British Home Stores and Marks and Spencer...

The shops were elegant, and there were a number of boutiques displaying the kind of clothes any woman would covet. Sarah paused before a small window displaying an enchanting outfit in rose-patterned cotton jersey.

Afterwards she decided that she had gone mad, but then it seemed the sensible thing to go into the shop, try on the outfit, buy it and part without a vestige of regret with more than half the money in her purse. She would need shoes to go with it, court shoes with high heels, and tights to match, and then, mindful of her shrinking wages, she made her way back to Marks and Spencer and found a sensible blue denim skirt and a couple of cotton tops to go with it. Undies used up almost all the money she had left; she ate a frugal lunch in a coffee-bar and took a bus back to Grosvenor Square. There was still a good deal of her day left, she thought happily as she walked down the quiet street where Lady Wesley lived, and it was a lovely day.

There was no one about as she went round the back of the house and went into her room. She fed Charles, took him into the garden for a stroll and then got out of her last year's dress and put on the new outfit. It did something for her, she decided happily, peering into the rather small looking-glass. She did her face, brushed out her hair and piled it tidily, put on the new shoes, bade Charles goodbye with a promised 'I'll be back for your supper,' and went out again, tripping through the tradesmen's entrance in her new shoes, feeling pleased with herself. She would go to the park and stroll around for a while. It would have been nice to have had someone to talk to...

She closed the door behind her, and stood a moment deciding which way to go and then set off, going quite slowly because of the new shoes.

CHAPTER FIVE

IT WAS the best part of a mile to Green Park, but
Sarah had the rest of the afternoon and evening to
herself, although she would go back in time for
supper. Lunch had been a scanty affair, and she
hadn't much more than the price of a cup of tea
with her. The pleasant feeling engendered by the
knowledge that she was looking her best made the
mile seem a good deal shorter than it was, and the
park, when she reached it, had few people in it.
She strolled along, glancing down with deep satisfaction at the rose-patterned skirt and the elegant
shoes. Indeed, she was so engrossed in their con-
templation that she walked into someone coming
towards her.

She knew at once who it was, for her nose was
within an inch of a vast expanse of waistcoat which
could only belong to the Professor. She said crossly,
'Oh, no...' and then, aghast at her own rudeness,
'Good afternoon, Professor Nauta.'

She detected mockery in his 'Good afternoon,
Miss Fletcher,' and his slow appraisal of her person.
'Well, well, it would be rude to say that I scarcely
recognise you, wouldn't it? Would it be appro-
priate for me to quote Chaucer? "And she was fair
as is the rose in May"...'

Sarah eyed him with dislike. 'Roses have thorns—
Shakespeare said that—and good day to you,

Professor. You are not only rude, you are unkind too.'

She looked up at him with her pansy eyes and met his hard gaze unwaveringly, and then was totally disarmed by his sudden smile. It was kind and friendly and contrite. 'Forgive me, Sarah, I am not sure what prompted me to speak to you like that. I wonder why, when we meet, I feel the urge to annoy you?'

'I have no idea,' said Sarah, trying to ignore the smile, her voice frosty, 'but I accept your apology, Professor. Goodbye.'

He put out a hand and held her firmly by one arm. 'Good, then could we cry truce for half an hour? Tea at Fortnum's, perhaps?'

She longed for tea. 'I think that you forget that you are asking the housemaid to have tea with you.'

He looked down his nose at her. 'My dear girl, I'll take my tea with anyone I choose. I am an ill-tempered, rude and impatient man, but I am not a snob.'

'In that case,' said Sarah, thinking of her tea, 'I'll accept.'

She made a splendid tea, and she had to admit afterwards that he had been a pleasant companion, not once fixing her with a cold eye or making nasty remarks, but carrying on the kind of conversation which put her quite at ease. Perhaps too much so, she thought uneasily, for he had remarked in the most casual of voices that having no family at all must make life lonely for her.

'Your father——?' he had asked gently, and she had told him that he had died several years earlier.

'And your mother?' She had told him too that her mother had died when she was in her teens.

'So you took over the housekeeping, I suppose?' His voice had been gentle.

'My father married again...'

He'd made a sympathetic noise. 'And your stepmother died and left you alone once more?'

'She still lives at my home,' she had answered. She remembered saying that now, and felt vexed that she had told him so much. Never for one moment did she imagine that he would have gone to the trouble to discover where her home was.

She changed out of her new outfit, hung it carefully away and went to her supper, where she detailed her day's activities without mentioning tea with Professor Nauta.

Lady Wesley was enjoying herself so much that she had decided to stay another week in town. Moreover, she intended to give a final party for her friends before she went. Beyond making known her wishes for this event, she left the actual arrangements to Mrs Butler, who in turn passed on the extra work to Parsons, Sarah and Kitty. The big reception-room on the first floor had to be polished and hoovered, flowers fetched, extra chairs brought in and the floor made ready for dancing. In the dining-room downstairs small tables had to be set up, extra china and glass found, silver polished and napkins and tablecloths starched and ironed. Of course, Cork presided over the entire undertaking, making his wishes known to the housekeeper who in turn instructed the rest of the staff. By the day of the party they were all tired, irritable and longing to get back to the country, especially Mudd, who had to put up with Lady Wesley's inability to make up her mind as to what she should wear.

There was to be a dinner party before most of the guests arrived with close friends and relations who lived in and around London. Sarah, helping Parsons with the table under the eagle eye of Cork, arranged the knives and forks and spoons just so, and rehearsed to herself what her duties would be during the evening. Cork had said that she was neat and quick enough to wait at table—she was to watch what Parsons did, look slippy with the vegetable dishes and be ready to take away the plates at the end of each course. 'And once the guests arrive, you are to circulate with your tray and be ready to help any lady who wishes to retire.'

'He means go to the loo,' whispered Parsons. 'You have to put down your tray and go upstairs with her and wait if she wants you to. Can't think why—a lot of fuss about nothing, if you ask me.'

There was to be no supper in the servants' hall; they were given high tea instead, and then told to go and put on their clean dresses and aprons ready for the evening. Miss Mudd had already gone upstairs to get Lady Wesley dressed, and Cook and Kitty were putting the finishing touches to the handsome dinner.

Sarah showered, let Charles into the garden, gave him his supper and started on the task of getting her abundant hair to lie smoothly on top of her head. This done, she pinned a clean, starched cap on it, surveyed as much of her person as she could in the looking-glass and went back to the house.

She could hear voices and laughter from the small
drawing-room behind the dining-room and, peeping
round the baize door into the hall, she watched
Cork, bearing a tray of drinks, make his stately way
to where Parsons was waiting. He turned to answer
the door once more, and Sarah whisked her head
inside to stand in a corner of the kitchen, waiting
for the gong.

At its first stroke, she nipped into the dining-
room and took her place beside the massive buffet.
Parsons was already at the other end of it and Cork
was at the door, holding it open for the company.
Lady Wesley, looking pleased with herself, swept
in with an elderly gentleman with a fierce mous-
tache, and her ten guests followed. The ladies all
looked very nice, thought Sarah, studying *haute
couture* at close quarters—which reminded her of
her own new clothes so that she smiled. But only
for a moment—a look of consternation came over
her face as the Professor entered, his handsome
head bent over a beautiful blonde girl wearing a
scarlet dress which Sarah, who was rather old-
fashioned, considered indecent. They sat down with
their backs to her and she sighed with relief. It was
unlikely that any of the guests would look at who
was serving them—they only saw a dish and a hand
holding it . . .

Parsons was serving the soup, and Cork was
occupied with the wines. Sarah changed her weight
from one leg to the other and listened to the cheerful
sound of people enjoying themselves. Strange to
think that ten years ago she would have been sitting
at table and someone else would have been standing
waiting to take away the plates. Cork's discreetly

modulated warning cough brought her back to the present. She slid around the table collecting the soup plates while the conversation hummed around her. She reached the girl in red satin—the dress wasn't decent, she could see right down her front ... She balanced the plate and stretched out an arm for the Professor's plate. He had turned to talk to his other neighbour, but he looked round before she could take the plate away and saw her, and then looked up into her face. Not a muscle of his features moved, and her ferocious stare dared him to so much as recognise her. All the same, she had the nasty feeling that he was laughing silently.

But she had taken the plunge now; she handed out *petits pois*, creamed spinach and carrot sticks, while Parsons went ahead of her with the new potatoes. When she reached the Professor she took great care not to look at any part of him. She concentrated on the spinach and tried not to see his large, well-kept hands as he helped himself.

Why should I be bothered about his hands? she asked herself as she replenished her dish for second helpings.

After that there were various sauces to hand round, plates to collect and cheese to offer and, since the other guests were expected very shortly, the coffee was served at the table too. She was waved away by Cork when she had taken round the coffee-cups, and went to stand by the buffet again until everyone got up to go upstairs. She joined the mad rush to get the table cleared, take the dishes down to the kitchen and collect the trays of canapés ready to offer once all the guests had arrived.

But before then she had to post herself at the foot of the staircase, ready to assist any lady who required help. Parsons was in the hall, taking cloaks and wraps as Cork admitted a constant stream of people, but presently the last of them had arrived, leaving her free to follow Parsons down to the kitchen. 'Cor, what a crowd,' said Parsons. 'Only hope they don't stay all night. My feet are killing me. I say, Sarah, what did you think of that girl in the red dress? The one next to Professor Nauta— I bet you a week's wages she hadn't got a thing on underneath...'

Sarah felt a certain satisfaction in agreeing with her.

The party went on for a long time—the last guest went some time after one o'clock in the morning. Miss Mudd, having spent the evening in the housekeeper's room drinking tea and reading *Woman's Own*, went grumbling upstairs to put Lady Wesley to bed. The Professor had left before midnight, called away to some emergency or other, and he had made no attempt to speak to Sarah—not that she would have welcomed that. She trotted to and fro clearing away the debris of the party, yawning her head off and longing for her bed. It was an hour later before she tumbled into it, too tired even for the cup of tea the cook had made for them all. Charles, pleased to see her again, climbed on to the divan and curled up beside her, and she was asleep within minutes.

It seemed only minutes when her alarm went off and she had to get up again.

They were returning to the country in two days' time, so there was a good deal to do. Sarah spent her scant leisure in the garden, nicely concealed behind the shrubs under her window, lying in the sun while Charles prowled to and fro.

They travelled back on the Saturday directly after breakfast, and she was delighted to be back in the country, although right at the back of her mind was the thought that she wasn't likely to see the Professor again. And the rest of the day was busy enough getting the house just so, ready for Lady Wesley who would arrive after lunch. They had their own midday meal first, and after the flurry of Lady Wesley's arrival they took a well-earned rest.

'And don't forget church in the morning,' warned Cork. 'And Sarah, Parsons wants the evening off tomorrow, so you'll have to make do with a free afternoon.' He paused to see what she would say, and when she said nothing at all, he went on, 'Half-past six, ready to lay up for supper and see to the rooms.'

She said, 'Yes, Mr Cork,' cheerfully enough; for some reason she was glad to be kept busy. She would go for a walk after her dinner on Sunday, she told herself, and shake off the feeling of despondency. She was tired, so were they all—in a day or so they would all settle down into their accustomed routine.

Charles, back in his own territory once more, lay passive in the yard behind her room, and presently she joined him, lying on the grass half-asleep.

Parsons had a boyfriend, which was why she wanted Sunday off. She told Sarah about him as they prepared the bedrooms for the night. Head porter at one of the big London hotels, she explained proudly, and they were going to marry in six months' time. 'Gets good tips,' said Parsons, 'and I hang on to almost all my wages. We've enough to put down on a nice little house close to Waterloo—handy for the tube—I'll get a part-time job. Shouldn't wonder if you don't get my job, Sarah. Mr Cork thinks highly of you, and even old Mudd likes you. Haven't you got a young man, then?'

'No—no, I haven't. I knew several boys—young men—when I was at home, but when I came to London I—I lost touch with them.'

'You'll find someone,' declared Parsons comfortably. 'Nice girl like you—too good for this job, too.' She paused expectantly, but Sarah had nothing to say so she went on, 'Not that you aren't a good worker. I bet you had a posh education. Mr Cork said he never had to tell you once how to lay up a table or explain how people like Lady Wesley live.'

Sarah folded a counterpane back very neatly. She smiled at Parsons. 'I'm very happy here with you all. I think of you as my friends, and I hope you don't mind.'

'Lor' bless you, of course not. Now, about tomorrow...'

Lady Wesley went to church in her car while the rest of them walked, for it was only ten minutes or so. The church was quite beautiful, its atmosphere redolent of great age, and the rector seemed almost as old. It was a pity that he preached such long sermons. Sarah sat between Miss Mudd and Parsons and allowed her mind to wander. She wondered what the Professor was doing with his

Sunday—at his home, wherever that was, perhaps out with friends, spending it with some pretty girl... She rose to her feet with everyone else and sang the last hymn. After lunch she would be free for a few hours. She would see to Charles, and then go for a walk—there were plenty of bridle-paths she could explore.

Mindful of Mr Cork's instructions, she presented herself at exactly half-past six in Mrs Legge's room. That lady was taking her ease with the Sunday papers and a glass of port.

'There you are,' she remarked unnecessarily. 'Well, Fletcher, you've had a few hours to yourself at any rate, and I'll see that you get some free time in the week to make up for your day off. Now go upstairs before you do anything else, and make up the bed in the Blue Room. Lady Wesley's niece is coming for supper and spending the night. Then get the table laid. Soup, cold salmon cutlets, salad, asparagus and potatoes on the side. Fruit and ice-cream, cheese and biscuits. They'll drink white wine. Mr Cork will check the table when you've finished. Off you go.'

The big house was quiet. Sarah nipped along to the Blue Room, her arms full of bed-linen, made up the bed, saw to the towels, checked soap and sponges and bath oils, fetched a handful of flowers from the garden and arranged them in a vase. It was strictly forbidden to cut any flowers without the gardener's permission, but there was no one about and the room looked so much nicer with the lilies of the valley and the early roses on the dressing-table. She closed the door and went smartly down to the dining-room. The leaves had been taken out of the vast table, but it was still far too big for three people. She began to arrange the linen and lace table-mats at one end. She was setting the cutlery just so when the half-open door was pushed wide open and the Professor walked in.

She frowned at the sudden delight she felt in seeing him, said with the politeness of a well-trained servant, 'Good evening, sir,' and rearranged the spoons. She felt light-headed with joy, and shaken just because he was standing there—she would think about that presently when she had the time. It would help matters if he said something instead of just standing there, doing nothing.

'Promotion?' he wanted to know blandly. 'Am I to congratulate you, Sarah?'

'No, Parsons has a day off.'

'And you, when do you have yours?'

'I had the afternoon part. Mrs Legge will let me have time off when I can be spared.' She clashed the knives in a pointed manner. 'You will excuse me, sir, I have to get the table laid.'

'Well, I can see that for myself,' he said reasonably. 'But don't expect me to believe that you can't do two things at once if you want to.'

'But I don't want to,' said Sarah.

He gave a short laugh. 'In that case, I'll go.' and he went.

There was no denying the fact that she was disappointed—which, considering she didn't like him, was unsettling.

Lady Wesley's niece arrived presently and Sarah, following Mr Cork's stately progress, took her coat and her case and went upstairs with them while she went into the drawing-room. Sarah could hear laughter from the half-closed door as she descended to the kitchen. The niece was pretty and beautifully dressed; perhaps she was the reason for the Professor's visit. Sarah drank the cup of tea Cook had ready for her, and listened carefully to Mr Cork's instructions.

Supper on Sundays was later than the usual dinner hour. Sarah took up her position by the sideboard as the last booming notes of the gong sounded. They were louder than usual—Mr Cork had had words with Knott and was taking it out on the gong, but nothing of his feelings showed on his face as he stood by the open door as Lady Wesley and her guests took their places at the table. The niece was seated facing Sarah, while the Professor sat with his back to her. The niece's name was Muriel de Foe-Burgess, and despite her prettiness she was insipid and, moreover, anxious to please. Sarah, shamelessly listening to the conversation as she handed out plates and took them away again, heard her agreeing with everything that was said so that the talk kept coming to a halt, for she contributed no remarks of her own. Although she became quite animated as she described, blow by blow, an episode from one of the soap operas on TV, since neither Lady Wesley nor the Professor had any idea of what she was talking about they could do nothing more than make polite murmurs. Sarah, observing the Professor's broad back closely, was quite sure that he was bored despite his beautiful manners. And why should I be so certain of that? she wondered, handing round the cheese.

The answer struck her like a thunderbolt as she watched him cutting a portion of Brie. It was so unexpected that the plate wobbled and he paused deliberately, not looking at her, and a good thing too for she had gone very pale and then red. Her insides were shaking like a jelly so that, contrary to Mr Cork's careful teaching, she had to steady the plate with her other hand. It was, she thought distractedly, the worst possible moment in which to discover that she was head over heels in love with him. She set the cheese back on the table and offered biscuits, and went to stand behind him again, dreamily admiring the back of his head, just for the moment perfectly content to mull over the sheer delight of her discovery.

She was recalled to her surroundings as Lady Wesley got up and sailed to the door. 'Coffee in the drawing-room, Cork,' she said as she left the room with Muriel and the Professor strolling behind, chatting pleasantly.

'And what happened to you, Fletcher?' Mr Cork wanted to know the moment they were alone. 'You of all people—I thought you were about to drop the cheese.'

'I'm sorry, Mr Cork, I felt giddy—only for a moment.'

'Well, don't do it again.' The reprimand was half-hearted—he had a soft spot for her and a sneaking feeling that she shouldn't be a housemaid at all. Indeed, as he had said to Mrs Legge on several occasions, Fletcher would look more at home sitting at the table and being waited on. 'You mark my words,' he had said, 'there's more to that girl than meets the eye.'

He went away to fetch the coffee-tray, and Sarah started to clear the table. She was crossing the hall

with a loaded tray when the Professor came out of
the drawing-room and saw her. Without a word he
took the tray from her, carried it down to the
kitchen where he dumped it on the table, and
walked away again, all the while silent. Sarah found
it unnerving.

Cork and Molly had been there, and Sarah was
hard put to it to satisfy their curiosity. It was Cork
who settled the matter when they chorused the
Professor's peculiar behaviour to him. 'Fletcher felt
giddy while she was serving the cheese. The
Professor, being a doctor, would have noticed.
Naturally, when he saw her with a loaded tray he
felt compelled to take it from her. If she had had
another giddy attack and dropped the tray and
smashed the Doulton and those crystal glasses,
Lady Wesley would have been very upset.' He added
severely, 'Replacements would have been stopped
out of your wages, Sarah. You'd have been poor
for months—years—to come.'

Sarah murmured contritely, and he added in a
fatherly way, 'Well, no harm's been done, anyway.'

Only to my heart, thought Sarah, and she started
to lay supper for them all.

She was tired by now, but since Parsons wasn't
back she would have to stay up until Miss de Foe-
Burgess went to her bed. She nipped over to feed
an indignant Charles, and then went back to sit in
the kitchen with Cook and Molly. None of them
had the urge to sit in the servants' hall; they sat
round the kitchen table, drinking tea and gos-
siping. Cork and Mrs Legge were in Mrs Legge's
sitting-room and the house was quiet.

It was almost eleven o'clock when the bell from the drawing-room rang and Sarah went up to answer it. Miss de Foe-Burgess was going to bed and wanted a glass of warm milk to be brought up to her room. Sarah said, 'Very good, miss,' in her meek housemaid's voice, and took care not to look at the Professor standing by the window.

'I'll ring when I'm ready,' said Muriel, not looking at Sarah. Her tinkling laugh, directed at the Professor no doubt, followed Sarah as she went back to the kitchen.

It was twenty minutes later before she was summoned to take up the milk. Muriel was sprawled on the bed, looking at a magazine. She didn't look up as Sarah went in. 'Put it on the table,' she said, and didn't answer Sarah's polite goodnight. It would have given Sarah great satisfaction to have poured the milk all over the girl's golden head.

But now she would be able to go to her own bed. She started down the staircase, which was forbidden territory during the daytime for the servants, but it was far quicker to get to the kitchen if she went down the main staircase to the hall. She went slowly, running her hand over the patina of the balustrade, feeling its ancient smoothness. She was almost at the bottom when she saw the Professor in the hall, watching her. It would have been cowardly to turn tail and run—besides, she longed to go to him. Not that she intended to do any such thing. She reached the bottom step and he was there, barring her way to the baize door.

He stared down at the frilly cap above her tired face. 'Afraid to look at me, Sarah?' he asked silkily.

She was too quick to say no, but she lifted her lovely eyes to his face and looked at him steadily. She said in a calm little voice, 'Goodnight, sir,' and felt his hands on her shoulders before he gathered her close and kissed her.

She could have stayed in his arms for ever. She made a small movement, and he released her at once and stood back so that she could pass him. She whisked away through the baize door and gained the kitchen, empty now save for Miss Mudd, waiting patiently for her ladyship to go to bed.

Her usually sour expression softened as she saw Sarah. 'Go to bed,' she said. 'You're worn out.'

Sarah made some rather wild reply and darted away to get into her bed and lie awake, despite her weariness, wondering what had possessed the Professor to behave the way he had. 'Totally out of character,' she muttered to Charles. 'And oh, if only he had meant it . . .'

Common sense returned with the morning. She took up Miss de Foe-Burgess's morning tea, since Parsons, after her day off, was having difficulty in coping with her morning chores. Sarah pulled back the curtains and let in the early morning sun, and the girl in the bed groaned and said sharply, 'Close the curtains, do. And bring me my breakfast in an hour.' She opened one eye. 'What is your name?'

'Fletcher, miss.'

Sarah picked up the small piles of clothing scattered around the room and went away, closing the door quietly behind her. If the Professor were to marry the lazy creature, it would break her heart.

She wanted him, above all things, to be happy, and that he could never be with Muriel de Foe-Burgess.

Of course, I could make him happy, she reflected, hurrying down the back stairs to her breakfast. He's ill-tempered and impatient and tiresome, but only sometimes... He'd loved his granny.

She was almost late; Mr Cork gave her a stern look before saying the grace he recited before meals, but he contradicted this before breakfast was over by remarking that Fletcher was filling out nicely. 'Mrs Legge and I never expected you would be able to undertake the tasks allotted to you,' he explained. 'But good food and hard work do wonders.'

Sarah spooned her porridge and, on the strength of the butler's remarks, helped herself to more milk.

Parsons was almost her old self again. 'I'll take up Miss de Foe-B's breakfast,' she said. 'She doesn't often come, thank goodness, for she makes enough work for two. I pity her husband when she gets one.'

'No need to get nasty,' reprimanded Mrs Legge. 'Though I must say, she'll make a bad wife for any man.'

'Got her claws into Professor Nauta? He was here to dine yesterday evening——'

Mr Cork coughed. 'We have no business discussing the guests in this house,' he observed ponderously. 'But I must admit that Miss de Foe-Burgess is not an ideal wife for a splendid man such as Professor Nauta. I fancy, though, that he is old enough and wise enough to know that for himself.'

They dispersed to their various jobs, and Sarah nipped across to give Charles his breakfast and allow him five minutes in the yard.

She repeated their breakfast conversation to his furry face, and he rumbled gently in reply. 'I wonder what he is doing now?' Sarah asked him, not needing to mention names. There was only one 'he' as far as she was concerned.

She would have been surprised if she had known. That surprise came to Sarah two days later when Cork sought her out as she hoovered the upstairs corridors. 'Her ladyship wishes to see you, Sarah. In the morning-room.'

Sarah followed him downstairs. Was it to be the sack? Had she done something unforgivable? Perhaps Miss de Foe-Burgess had complained...

Lady Wesley was seated in an armchair by the window. She answered Sarah's 'Good morning, my lady,' with a nod, and adjusted her spectacles.

'I have had a letter from Mevrouw Nauta, and before you say anything I should make it clear that I know that you have been to Holland and have met her. She is coming to England for a few weeks for a rest, after the rather trying time that she had—you are aware of that, of course... and by the strangest coincidence she asked if I had any idea of your whereabouts. She will need a companion while she is here, and would like to have you. Much as I am loath to part with you, Fletcher, I am delighted that I can send you to her.'

She paused, and Sarah said quietly, 'I would prefer not to go, Lady Wesley, and if I might suggest, surely Parsons would be more suitable?'

'Parsons would not do at all. Besides, she is engaged to be married, as you know, and is able to meet her fiancé easily while she is here.'

Lady Wesley drew herself up. 'Anyway, I telephoned Mevrouw Nauta as soon as I had read her letter, and told her that I would send you when she arrives at the end of the week.' She glanced at the letter in her hand. 'Mevrouw Nauta says that she will be over here for about a month, and of course you will return here and resume your duties when she goes.' She folded the letter. 'You will be a companion to Mevrouw Nauta, a position I am persuaded is more suitable to your upbringing than that of housemaid.' She nodded. 'You may go.'

Sarah went, fuming. 'In this day and age,' she muttered as she went back upstairs. 'Being ordered around just as though I were a—servant...' On the other hand, it would be nice to live a normal life again and not wear a cap and apron. And she would see the Professor, although that might be unwise. She finished her work and went to the kitchen to have her elevenses, and took the opportunity of telling everyone there what Lady Wesley had said. She had expected tart rejoinders, but instead they were all delighted.

'Just up your street,' declared Parsons, and Cork said ponderously, 'It has always been obvious to us all here, Sarah, that you weren't one of us. I have nothing to say against your work—you are an excellent worker—but there are certain things... You are not perhaps aware that you have always addressed Lady Wesley as such, instead of "my lady" or, when referred to, as "her ladyship"—a small

matter, but one which Mrs Legge and I were quick
to notice.'

'Oh, dear,' said Sarah, 'do forgive me, Mr
Cork—don't hold it against me.'

'Certainly not, Sarah. You have been, and are
still, one of us, a valued colleague.'

Sarah put down her cup. 'Oh, Mr Cork, that's
one of the nicest things anyone has ever said to me.
I've been so happy with you all.' She beamed round
the table. 'I'll be so pleased to see you all again.'

'You'll be sure of a warm welcome from us,' said
Mr Cork, and everyone murmured an echo to his
words.

There was the question of Charles, of course,
settled immediately by Lady Wesley. He was to go
with Sarah; Cork conveyed the news to her on the
following evening. 'And there's a retired maid
coming to fill your place until you come back,' he
told her. 'A pleasant body, left to get married some
years ago, but is now widowed and glad of a job.'

'It is extraordinary,' remarked Sarah to an at-
tentive Charles, 'how things turn out, but I'm not
sure if I'm glad or not—you see, I'll probably see
him, which will be lovely—but on the other hand,
I'm not sure...'

The Professor wasn't sure, either. It had all taken
a bit of arranging, and his mother, knowing him
well, had raised no objection to his suggestion that
a few weeks' holiday in England might do her good.
'You will not need to be lonely,' he assured her.
'You remember Sarah, who looked after
Grandmother so well? She is working for Aunt

Beatrice, and she is quite willing to be your companion while you are in England.'

Mevrouw rapidly put two and two together and made five. 'Why, Radolf, that would be delightful. Such a nice, quiet, unassuming girl, exactly the kind of person I would have chosen. Minster Lovell will be lovely, and the rest will do me so much good.'

The Professor bade his parent goodbye and hung up. 'It is ridiculous,' he observed to Trotter, who was lying across his feet, 'that I find the girl so disturbing, and this must be put right at once. I will see as much as possible of her during the next few weeks, and thereby prove that my interest in her is both nonsensical and transitory.'

Trotter thumped her tail in agreement—she couldn't understand the long words, but she got the gist.

It occurred to Sarah when she woke the next morning that no one had told her where she was to go, and she had quite forgotten to ask, but at breakfast Mrs Legge told her. 'Minster Lovell, near Burford. Knott is to drive you there; it's not all that far. I dare say he'll take you through Buckingham and Witney. Pretty country there. You'll do your work as usual, Sarah, but I'll excuse you your evening duties before you go so that you can pack your things.' She added comfortably, 'Leave anything you don't want in your room, packed up in a case.'

The week ended and Sarah packed her things, was sent for by Lady Wesley to be given last-minute instructions, and was waved on her way by her domestic companions. She got into the car beside

Knott, with Charles sitting philosophically in his basket on the back seat. She was to be at the house before Mevrouw Nauta arrived, so that the housekeeper could show her round and she would be familiar with her surroundings.

'I wish I knew a little more,' she said worriedly to Knott as they drove away, and was comforted by his,

'Don't you worry, Sarah—it'll make a nice change from sweeping and dusting.'

CHAPTER SIX

MINSTER LOVELL, when they reached it, was charming, with its river winding through the village. The cottages were built of Burford stone, some thatched, some stone-roofed. Knott drove up its street, past a large, handsome house at the top and then, half a mile further on, turned in through a wide gateway, drove up the short, curved drive and stopped before a low, rambling house with an irregular stone roof, its walls almost hidden by climbing roses, honeysuckle, clematis and ivy. The garden around it was informal, and it was sheltered by a variety of trees. It reminded Sarah of her own home, and she said with real pleasure, 'Oh, Mr Knott, what a delightful house.'

He was unloading her case and Charles. 'Very nice—nice inside, too. We'll go in the side door.'

A good thing he had said that, for she was on the point of ringing the front doorbell. She said rather breathlessly, 'Oh, sorry—I wasn't thinking,' and followed him round the side of the house and in through a stout door.

A stone passage brought them to the kitchen, and as they went Knott raised his voice. 'Mrs Boot? Are you there, Mrs Boot?'

A small, piping voice answered him, and he opened a door at the end of the passage and motioned Sarah to go past him. The kitchen was exactly as she would have wished it to be, with its flagstoned floor, an Aga along one wall, and huge dresser and great scrubbed table in the centre flanked by Windsor chairs. There was a cat by the Aga, and a trio of kittens in a basket.

The elderly woman at the table was short and stout with a round, happy face. She said cosily, 'There you are, then, Mr Knott and the young lady too. Sit down and have coffee. You'll be wanting to get back I dare say, Mr Knott, and that'll leave us in peace to go over the house together, Miss...?'

'Fletcher, Mrs Boot, but I'd like it if you would call me Sarah.'

'Well, now, Sarah's a pretty name.' Mrs Boot poured coffee and cut generous slices of cake. 'There's still an hour or so before Mevrouw Nauta comes—lunch, she said, and that means half-past one. I'll show you your room and then take you round the house, so's you'll know your way around.'

She looked at Sarah with twinkly blue eyes. 'It's quiet here, love, but I dare say you're country-bred?'

Sarah nodded. 'Yes, I am, though I lived in London for quite a few years.'

'Nasty old place,' declared Mrs Boot comfortably, and gave Mr Knott more cake. 'You're all just back, I hear.'

Knott launched into an account of their weeks in London, which lasted until he declared that he would have to go. 'And I'll be back for you, Sarah, soon as Mevrouw Nauta goes back to Holland.' He grinned at her. 'Make the most of it, you and Charles.'

'Ah, yes, your little cat,' observed Mrs Boot. 'We'll let him sit here for a bit with my Flo, and see how they get on together.'

Freed from his basket, Charles prowled stealthily round the kitchen, eyed by Flo. He came presently to stand beside her and, after a moment, to Sarah's relief, sat down with every appearance of peaceful intent.

'That's all right, then,' said Mrs Boot cheerfully. 'We'll go upstairs.'

Sarah's room was at the back of the house, overlooking a large garden which merged into the fields beyond. She stood at the window for a moment, delighting in the view. The garden was informal, with ornamental trees and shrubs interspersed with clumps of flowers with paths in between. She turned away to listen to her companion, who was chatting about the room. It was pretty, well furnished and the adjoining bathroom was all that a girl could ask for. 'And Mevrouw Nauta's room is on the other side of the landing, Miss Sarah. I'll just show you. You put your coat on the bed and we'll take a look round.'

'It's lovely, Mrs Boot,' said Sarah, and spied a door leading on to a small balcony. 'Could Charles be up here with me? He's used to being with me all the time, especially at night.'

'Of course he can, Miss Sarah——'

They were crossing the landing and Sarah stopped for a moment. 'Thank you, Mrs Boot, but please don't call me Miss Sarah, just Sarah. I'm the housemaid at Lady Wesley's.'

'Housemaid you may be, Miss Sarah, but I know a lady when I see one.' Mrs Boot opened a door and stood aside for Sarah to go in. The room was charming, quite large and rather low-ceilinged, its furniture a golden mahogany with thick carpeting underfoot and pale chintz curtains at the long windows. They went from it presently to inspect the other rooms on that floor, and then climbed to the rooms above. 'And I've a flat all to myself at the end there,' pointed out Mrs Boot. 'There's only me living in, though there's two women from the village who come each day to see to the housework. There's a gardener and a boy, too——' She paused. 'There's a car coming up the drive now—far too early for Mevrouw Nauta.' She started down the stairs. 'We'd best go and see...'

As they went, Sarah asked, 'This house—is it Mevrouw Nauta's?'

'Oh, no—didn't anyone tell you?' Mrs Boot had gained the landing and was peering over the gallery banisters. 'There, I might have known...'

She bustled down the stairs with Sarah hard on her heels, just as the door opened and Mevrouw Nauta came in with the Professor behind her.

Sarah stood poised halfway down, crushing a strong wish to turn tail and run upstairs again while at the same time filled with the delight of the sight of him. But common sense took over, she descended into the hall at a decorous pace and waited to be spoken to.

Mrs Boot, who had greeted Mevrouw Nauta and received, very much to Sarah's surprise, a hug and a kiss from the Professor, turned to smile at her. 'Here's Miss Sarah, got here an hour ago. We've just been looking over the house.'

'So nice to see you again,' declared Mevrouw Nauta. 'And now, tell me how you are—you look so well; you were far too thin... And how providential that Lady Wesley should have you in her household.' She looked at her son. 'Isn't it marvellous, Radolf?'

He said coolly, 'Hello, Sarah. I'm sure you will look after my mother. Boots, dear, I do have to get back to town, so could we have lunch as soon as possible?' He looked at his mother. 'You wouldn't object, my dear?'

'Of course not, Radolf. Sarah, come upstairs with me while I tidy myself. Radolf, pour us a drink, will you, we will be less than five minutes.'

Sarah hadn't said a word—she hadn't really had the chance. She followed Mevrouw Nauta upstairs and into her room, and the lady said, 'I shall have a nap after lunch, and that will give you a chance to get to know the house. It's rather lovely, isn't it? My mother left it to Radolf, and he likes to spend his weekends here.'

So that accounted for the high-handed way he had asked to have lunch earlier, thought Sarah. Someone might have told her, although, on second thoughts, she really had no right to expect anyone to tell her anything.

She unzipped Mevrouw Nauta's small travelling-case and handed out comb and powder and lipstick, opened all the windows while Mevrouw Nauta was in the bathroom and took a quick peep at herself in the looking-glass. She wasn't looking her best, but that was because she was uncertain as to what happened next. Was she on the same level as

Mrs Boot, or was she to have her meals in the dining-room, and should she ask?

She didn't need to. The Professor was in the hall, surrounded by his mother's luggage. He said, 'You'll come to the drawing-room for drinks, Sarah, and have your meals with my mother. You may be an efficient housemaid, but in this house you are my mother's companion.'

He didn't smile, and his voice was as detached as his manner. There seemed no point in replying to him. She went past him, following Mevrouw Nauta as she swept into the drawing-room and took a chair by the french windows, which were open on to the garden. 'Come and sit by me, Sarah,' she commanded. 'I believe that I am going to enjoy my stay here. Do you drive a car?'

Sarah accepted a glass of sherry. 'Well, I can drive—I have a licence, but I haven't driven for years.'

'It's quiet round here,' said Mevrouw Nauta expansively. 'We shall be able to go for nice little drives, Radolf. Is that Mini still in the garage?'

'Yes, Wills——' Wills was the gardener '—uses it from time to time. There is no reason why Sarah shouldn't drive it. It's easy, and as you say the roads around here are fairly quiet. I might suggest that she takes it out on her own until she is confident that she can manage it.'

Sarah took a sip of sherry and ground her teeth with temper. The Professor was obviously bent on being his nastiest self. Well, he could needle her as much as he wanted to. She remembered his kiss and her face flamed, and he watched the soft colour flood over her ordinary face, transforming it into prettiness.

Lunch was leisurely and elegant, and so was the conversation. The Professor, a practised host, eased her into their talk with an evanescent skill, touching upon one impersonal topic after another so that presently she lost her stiffness and began to enjoy herself. So that when, as they rose from the table and Mevrouw Nauta declared that she was going to her room to take a nap and that Sarah was to amuse herself until teatime, her son remarked that it might be a good idea if he were to show Sarah round the gardens before he went, Sarah was perfectly amenable. It was hard to imagine that this pleasant man with beautiful manners was the same impatient and irritable one who seemed to dog her footsteps. Not that that mattered—she supposed that she would love him forever, bad temper and all.

It was obvious within minutes that he loved his home, and when they had strolled round the grass paths, discussed the display of flowers and stood by the clear, narrow stream running through one corner of the grounds, he took her to the cluster of outbuildings behind the house. The stables held a donkey, living out his days in peace, an elderly horse that used to draw the cart Wills favoured when he fetched stores from Witney, and a gentle pony. 'Mother has a small governess-cart. She likes to drive herself round the local lanes,' explained the Professor. There were two cats and a nondescript dog sleeping in the yard, and as the Professor stopped to pat the beast Sarah asked, 'You said you had a dog, didn't you? Why didn't you bring her with you? Doesn't she like the country?'

'Trotter loves it. She's at the vet's being trimmed and generally looked over. I'll bring her with me next time.'

'Do you come often?' she asked, and wished that she hadn't when he answered, after a pause,

'Whenever I can,' in a cool voice which abruptly warned her not to ask any more questions.

They were walking back to the house, and she said matter-of-factly, 'If you don't mind, I think that I should go and unpack so that I'm ready for Mevrouw Nauta. Thank you for showing me the garden, it's beautiful.'

She smiled up into his unsmiling face, wishing that she was beautiful and rich and exquisitely dressed and knew how to make him smile. She gave a little nod and walked away after a moment, for he had nothing to say.

Charles had gone to sleep on the balcony but he opened one eye as she went in. 'We'll go down to the garden presently,' she promised him, 'but I must wait until Radolf's gone. I wonder when he'll come again? Because if he does, I must do my best not to be here.' She picked up the cat and he sat in her arms, purring. 'I would like him to be here,' she explained, 'but it won't do. He doesn't like me. I've done my best, but I'm too ordinary.' She gave a great sigh. 'He does need a wife so badly—if only I were different, I would do nicely.' She gave a great sniff, put Charles down and opened her case.

By the middle of the week she was forced to admit that Mevrouw Nauta really didn't need a companion. She enjoyed perfect health, was never at a loss for something to do and would, Sarah considered, have been perfectly happy by herself. All the same, life was very pleasant, for they enjoyed the same things: gardening when Wills allowed them to, driving the pony and trap around the narrow lanes, playing Demon Patience in the evenings, listening to the vast selection of records in the small sitting-room with the doors open on to the garden. Once Sarah had got over her initial uncertainty, they talked like old friends.

Mevrouw Nauta, probing gently into Sarah's life, liked what she heard, and in her turn let fall an occasional tit-bit about her son. 'I become quite worried,' she stated untruthfully, 'for Radolf works too hard. It is ten years since he was jilted by a most unsuitable girl, and he seems to think that all women are as faithless as she was. So like a man, my dear. Still, I have high hopes that he will marry soon.'

They were having tea in the garden, and Sarah put her cup back in its saucer with a sudden jerk which sounded too loud in the rural quiet around them. 'Oh? That will be nice for him—for them both,' she said inanely.

Mevrouw Nauta, sitting upright in her chair, spoke cheerfully. 'Yes, Sarah, it should be very nice. And it will last— Radolf is not an impetuous man, he will be very sure.'

She handed her cup for more tea. 'These scones are delicious, I'll have another. You are not bored here? You must have a free day each week. Do you wish to go shopping or go to a cinema or visit friends?' She gazed at Sarah and added carelessly,

'Radolf will be down late on Saturday, and he will spend Sunday here. We might all go for a drive...'

Sarah bent to stroke Charles, who had come into the garden to sit beside her. 'Would you mind if I had Sunday off, Mevrouw Nauta? I don't need to buy anything, but I met the vicar yesterday and he asked me to go to lunch after church. He has several children, and he thought we might have a walk and a picnic tea...'

Which was almost true for she had been invited, but the invitation had been a vague suggestion and certainly not for Sunday. Her companion agreed readily. 'How pleasant for you. We shall be coming to church with you, of course.' A remark which sent Sarah into a flat spin.

The week inched its way to Saturday and Sarah, despite her good resolutions, had washed her hair, done her nails and taken great pains with her face. She would have liked to have put on the new rose-patterned outfit, but that might have looked as though she was trying to get the Professor's attention. She got into the better of her cotton dresses and discovered that she need not have bothered, for by ten o'clock that evening he hadn't arrived.

'Don't wait up, Sarah,' said Mevrouw Nauta. 'If you would just go along to the kitchen and ask Mrs Boot to make sandwiches and leave some coffee on the Aga, and perhaps a bowl of fruit with the sandwiches, and put my room ready as usual? Oh, and pop into Radolf's room and see that the bed is turned down and so on. Goodnight, Sarah.'

Dismissed and disappointed, Sarah found Mrs Boot, gave her the messages and accepted a cup of tea, which she drank as she listened to Mrs Boot's complaints about her varicose veins with real sympathy. 'Not that I should complain,' said Mrs Boot. 'Mr Radolf, he's forever asking me how my legs are—I've had them done once, had a room all to myself and ever such kind nurses—up at St Cyprian's, that was. Such a dear little boy,' she reminicsed. 'Not good, mind you, always up to mischief, but he loved his old nanny—he always said when he came home from school for the holidays that when he was a grown man I should look after his house for him. And he kept his promise. I know he's got a house in London, and a very nice one too, but this is his home. Time he married.' She beamed at Sarah. 'You go off to bed, love, I'll see to the sandwiches.'

Sarah, lying awake, heard the car drive up soon after midnight. She turned over and went to sleep then; she would see him at breakfast.

She was downstairs as usual in time to help Mrs Boot bring in the splendid breakfast Mevrouw Nauta enjoyed. She was arranging the hot-plate on the sideboard when that lady came in.

Her good morning was brisk and cheerful. 'Radolf has had his,' she told Sarah. 'He has gone for a walk, and he will be back in time for church.' She talked on so that Sarah had little need to answer, and presently she went away to get ready for church and Sarah cleared the table. The daily women didn't come on Sunday and, although Mrs Boot had never asked for help, Sarah knew she was grateful for it.

There was time to make the beds and tidy the bedrooms and bathrooms before Sarah, in the rose-patterned dress, went downstairs again.

The Professor was in the hall faultlessly turned out, sitting in one of the armchairs reading a newspaper. He glanced up as she reached the bottom step and got to his feet, looking her over. 'Very nice,' he commented blandly. 'For my benefit?'

She said pointedly, 'Good morning, Professor Nauta. I have my day off. I am going out to lunch after I have been to church.'

He raised his eyebrows. 'That's quick work.' His mother came down the stairs then, and he went on, 'But let us by all means go to church first.'

They went in his car, and in church she found herself sitting between mother and son. She said her prayers and sang the hymns in a small, sweet voice, and didn't hear a word of the sermon. She was too busy wondering how she could contrive to slip away after the service without her companions knowing that she wasn't going to the vicarage.

Kindly fate was on her side. As they left their pew, Mevrouw Nauta spied friends. 'The Saunders,' she said to her son. 'We should go and speak to them.' And so Sarah was able to slip away and mingle with the small crowd round the church door and then take herself off.

Pleasure at the ease with which she had got away didn't last long. She had no idea where to go. To stay near the village wouldn't do at all—she might be seen, and although the pub stood invitingly open, she didn't dare go in. The village was a chatty place, and sooner or later someone would pass on the news that she had been seen in the village when she should have been at the vicarage. Without appearing to do so she studied the signpost at the village centre. She didn't want to go to Brize Norton—Swinbrook sounded all right, and she remembered that Mrs Boot had said something about a small wood there. She walked off briskly. She was wearing the wrong shoes for a country walk, but there was no help for it. Once she was out of sight of the village she slowed her pace; she had the rest of the day and it was only a mile or two. The country was gently hilly and well wooded, and she strolled along, thinking about the sandwiches she would eat presently and the glass of lemonade to go with them. She would stay out for tea as well, she decided, and opened the pochette she had taken to church. She had more than enough money with her...

There was a twopenny piece and five pence hiding away under her hanky, and nothing else. She remembered that she had hurriedly thrust a hanky and some money into her pochette just before she left her room—she hadn't counted it because Mevrouw Nauta had wanted her for something. 'Fool,' she said out loud. Seven pence wouldn't buy her anything at all. She would have to find somewhere to rest and then go back—there was nothing else to do.

She walked on for a little way until the lane narrowed between woods, and presently she saw a likely spot. A hillock, quite near the lane, nicely shaded and covered in grass and moss. There was a tree to lean against too, and she made herself comfortable with her back to the lane, closed her eyes and, since there was nothing else to do, went to sleep.

It was very quiet in the wood and there was nothing to disturb her. She woke several hours later and sat up. The Professor was sitting beside her; he had discarded his exquisitely tailored grey suit and was wearing elderly slacks and an open-necked shirt. He wasn't looking at her and his profile looked to her to be an ill-tempered one.

She gave a tentative cough and said, 'Hello,' in a rather small voice, and he turned his head.

'What in the devil's name do you think you're doing?' he harshly demanded.

'You should watch your language, Professor,' said Sarah severely. 'And it's none of your business.'

'I will use whatever language I want to, and I choose to make it my business. What in heaven's name possessed you to tell a string of lies about lunching at the vicarage——?'

She interrupted him. 'How did you find out? And they weren't quite lies—the vicar said he would ask me to have lunch, but he didn't say when.'

'So why pretend you were going there today?' His eyes were blue steel, and she suppressed a shiver. And, when she didn't answer, 'Because I was at home?'

'Well, yes, I suppose so.'

'I see. In future, arrangements will be made for your day off when I am here so that there will be no need for us to meet.' He glanced at her. 'Will that suit you?'

She wanted to agree with dignity, but instead she felt her throat close over tears, which were going to burst into a flood at any moment. Everything had gone wrong: he was cold-hearted and mean and arrogant and she loved him to distraction and far worse, for the moment at any rate, she was famished. The tears had their way, and she wailed in a miserable hiccup, 'I'm so very hungry...'

He put an arm round her and offered his handkerchief. 'I would imagine you would be,' he observed reasonably, 'since it is almost four o'clock. Now, dry your eyes and tidy yourself and we will find somewhere for tea.'

His voice sounded different now, unhurried and friendly and just sufficiently sympathetic. She supposed that that was how he spoke to his patients. She mopped her face and put a hand up to her hair.

'Oh, hopeless,' said the Professor. 'Take it down and tie it back.' He fished in a pocket and handed her a piece of string. 'Here, turn round.'

'Thank you, you are very kind, but you don't need to ask me to tea, I'll go back—I must explain to Mevrouw Nauta. Is she very angry?'

'Not in the least, although she did wonder why you went to such lengths.'

She gave a final sniff. 'Do I look awful?'

'I have seen you looking better.'

A reply which annoyed her very much. 'I am afraid I have spoilt your afternoon,' she said haughtily. 'Do please go to—to wherever it was you were going.'

'I was looking for you. Not a difficult task—that dress shows up for miles.' He got to his feet and held out a hand. 'Come along.' He whistled and Trotter appeared from the bushes, gave a pleased bark at the sight of Sarah, and accompanied them to the car. The dog got into the back and stood leaning her head between them as the Professor

drove away. He didn't go far—a mile or two down
the lane to the next village, where he stopped outside
a small, cosy-looking pub. He offered no information and Sarah, urged to get out, did so without
demur. The three of them walked round to the back
of the pub and went in through a side door. The
kitchen was comfortably furnished and lived-in,
with an old-fashioned gas oven against one wall and
a great stone sink under the far window. There was
an elderly woman sitting at the table, and the
Professor said, 'Hello, Meg, may we come to tea?'

She looked very like Mrs Boot, and Sarah wasn't
surprised when he said, 'This is Mrs Prior, Mrs
Boot's sister and an old friend. Miss Fletcher and
I are longing for something to eat.'

'Bless you, Mr Radolf, there's the kettle on the
boil and one of my fruit cakes.' She studied Sarah's
woebegone face and added, 'And if you're hungry,
I've just collected some eggs—a nice boiled egg,
perhaps, and some of my scones and jam and
cream.'

The Professor planted a kiss on her round cheek.
'Bless you, Meg, it sounds delightful. May we have
it here with you? Where's Dick?'

'Gone over to Smallbone's farm to get some of
his bacon.' While she was talking she was setting
cups and saucers and plates on the table. 'Sit down
while I boil the eggs. Home for the weekend, are
you? And how's London?' She smiled at him.
'When you were a little boy you always said you'd
never live there.'

'Beggars can't be choosers,' said the Professor
gravely.

'Go on with you, Mr Radolf, you're no beggar, though I suppose there's not much work for you in these parts.' She glanced at Sarah, and said, 'You'll be the young lady companion for Mevrouw Nauta, Miss, my sister was telling me...'

Sarah smiled rather shyly, out of her depth. The Professor had seemed so angry when she had first woken up, and now here he was chatting away to this nice, comfortable soul as though he had known her all his life.

Uncannily hitting the nail on the head, he said now, 'Mrs Boot was my nanny, Sarah, and I've known her and Meg ever since I can remember.' He saw her frown. 'Oh, you're wondering why that should be when I was born and brought up in Holland. We always came over to my grand-mother's house, which is now mine, for school hol-idays. I suppose that eventually I shall return to my home in Holland and follow the same pattern with my own children.'

A remark which saddened her—he watched the sadness reflected in her face, and his eyes were no longer steely but a bright blue. He said easily, 'Do you know this part of the world at all?'

She shook her head, and he began a rambling colloquy which needed no replies, and when Meg brought the eggs and poured their tea the talk was all of local happenings and Dick's rheumatics. Very much cheered by Meg's splendid tea, Sarah began to feel a great deal better. She had been silly, she could see that now, and the Professor had been very nice about it. All the same, she would avoid him in the future. There was a side to him which she was only just beginning to discover—under that cold, impersonal manner was someone quite different and exciting.

She finished her tea, thanked Meg nicely and got back into the car. She sat silently, rehearsing what she would say to Mevrouw Nauta. She supposed she would have supper with them, but she could plead a headache directly after.

They went into the house together with Trotter bounding ahead, and Sarah went at once to the sitting-room where Mevrouw Nauta liked to sit and write her letters. At the door she paused and looked back at the Professor, standing in the hall still. 'Thank you for—for finding me,' she said. 'You've been very kind.'

She didn't much care for his smile. She drew a heartening breath and opened the door.

Mevrouw Nauta made light of the matter. 'Oh, I quite understand,' she told Sarah, 'and it was most thoughtful of you to give us the opportunity to spend the day together. It was only by chance that Radolf discovered that you weren't at the vicarage and that you had been seen going towards Swinbrook. You poor child, your day off hasn't been very successful. We must do better next week.'

That left supper to get through, thought Sarah as she went to her room. She stayed there until the very last minute, sitting on her bed thinking about the Professor. He wasn't likely to come again until the weekend, and she would have to think of something before then so that they wouldn't need to meet. It was a lowering thought, but at least she would see him for another few hours.

When she went down to the drawing-room with barely two minutes before the gong would sound and no time for a drink, Mevrouw Nauta was alone. 'There you are, Sarah, come and keep me company. I always feel lonely when Radolf goes away.'

Sarah perched on a chair. 'Oh—he's gone?'

'Why, yes, my dear. Unexpectedly—he phoned someone or other and told me that he would have to drive up to London straight away.'

Which serves me right, thought Sarah, but he'll come again, and even if I only see him for a minute or two...

Not even for a minute or two, as it turned out. There was no sign of him at the next weekend, nor for the following one either, and at the end of the week Mevrouw Nauta was to return to Holland. Sarah, who took her duties seriously, drove her employer through the surrounding countryside in the car, accompanied her in the pony trap, gardened under her direction when old Wills allowed it, and commented suitably on Mevrouw Nauta's flow of conversation. She fetched and carried, too, found lost library books, unpicked knitting, discussed clothes and generally made herself useful.

The last day came, and she packed for the pair of them. Knott was to fetch her during the morning and the Professor, said his mother vaguely, was sending someone to collect her and drive her to his London home. 'He will go back with me for a few days. His father will be glad to see him.' She said happily, 'I have so enjoyed my little holiday, Sarah, and you have been a delightful companion. I shall miss you. I hope we shall see something of each other...'

'I expect I shall be with Lady Wesley,' said Sarah, 'and I dare say you visit her sometimes?'

'Indeed I do.' She paused, listening. 'I think that is Knott, come to fetch you.'

'I ought to wait and see you safely on your way,' began Sarah, and stopped as the door opened and the Professor came in.

He bade them good morning, kissed his mother and looked at Sarah. 'Knott is outside if you're ready, Sarah. Thank you for looking after my mother so well.' He opened the door again, and she shook Mevrouw Nauta's hand and smiled rather uncertainly at them both as she went past him to the hall where Mrs Boot was waiting.

'There, now,' said that good-natured soul. 'I'm sorry to see you go, Miss Sarah. A real help you've been.'

Sarah shook hands again, and went outside to find Knott by the car, which was standing side by side with the Professor's. She wished with her whole heart that the Professor hadn't come; he had dismissed her like a stranger, and she supposed miserably that that was how she would remember him.

She wished Knott a polite good morning, put Charles in his basket into the back of the car and then got in beside Knott. Mrs Boot was at the door waving, and she waved back as Knott asked, 'Had a good time, have you? Plenty of work for you when you get back. Parsons is off sick and Mrs Willis, who came in your place, had to go home yesterday—her mother is ill.'

Oh, well, perhaps hard work would answer her problem—there'd be no time to think. She looked back as they reached the end of the drive. The Rolls was just leaving the house. Knott gave her a quick glance. 'Sorry to be coming back?'

'Oh, no. I've enjoyed being here, but I missed you all, Mr Knott.'

He gave a satisfied grunt, echoed in various ways by the others when they reached Lady Wesley's house. Her room was ready for her, said Mrs Legge, and a nice hot dinner and, in the meantime, there was tea in the pot.

After dinner it was work; it was hoped that Parsons would be back within the next few days, but until then Sarah would be required to do the work of two, and although everyone was willing to give what help they could, it was no good expecting Mr Cork to make beds or Mrs Legge to polish brass doorknobs. Well, thought Sarah, I wanted hard work and now I've got it. Just for a moment she allowed herself to wallow in self-pity. 'I don't suppose he ever thinks of me, even with dislike,' she moaned at Charles, who yawned and turned his back.

She was wrong—the Professor was thinking of her, sitting in his mother's drawing-room, and although he had said nothing at all that lady remarked casually, 'I wonder how little Sarah is getting on? I cannot think why she must work as a housemaid. Surely, you could have helped her to a more suitable job, Radolf?'

'Of course I could. She's an obstinate girl with a low opinion of me, and I can assure you that I have tried to discover a means whereby she gets more suitable employment without discovering that I am the source. If she knew that, she would refuse immediately.' He added bitterly, 'At least I know where she is.'

'Yes, dear,' said his mother placidly. 'What kind of job had you in mind?'

'I have no idea, Mother. The obstinate little fool, dusting and making beds and opening doors...'

He sounded savage, and his parent judged it prudent to say nothing to this outburst. He was very like his father, she reflected lovingly, with the same fierce temper, allowed only to surface fairly infrequently when their feelings got too much for their iron control. Presently she said soothingly, 'Can you stay for a day or two, Radolf, or must you go back to London? Your father is hoping that you would go sailing with him.'

He was his usual calm self again. 'I can spare a couple of days. Is the boat down at Sneek?'

'Yes, dear. He will be pleased. Shall I ask a few friends in while you are at home? The van Dongens are back from France...'

He had gone to stand by the window. 'Oh, yes? They've been on holiday?'

'Yes, dear. And Lisa—the eldest girl—you remember her, so pretty and witty, has returned with them. She has that splendid job—something at an embassy, I think. Highly thought of and much sought after.'

He glanced at her over his shoulder. 'Lisa? As hard as nails and talks too much!'

A remark which pleased his mother enormously—as soon as he he had gone she had a long and satisfying conversation on the telephone with Lady Wesley.

CHAPTER SEVEN

PARSONS didn't come back as soon as Mrs Legge had hoped. Sarah had to forgo her day off, something she did with outward cheerfulness since there was no point in complaining; but when Parsons returned halfway through the following week, Mrs Legge sent for Sarah.

'You've been a good girl, not complaining at all at the extra work and no day off. You may have Sunday and Monday free and, since Knott is going to go up to town on Monday morning early and come back in the evening, Mr Cork and I think that you should go with him for a treat. He'll put you down wherever you want, and arrange to pick you up in the early evening.' And, when Sarah opened her mouth, she said, 'No, you have no need to thank me, it is your just due. You can enjoy a nice day shopping or visiting friends.'

Sarah said meekly, 'Yes, Mrs Legge, and thank you and Mr Cork, it is very kind of you,' for although she had no wish to go to London, it was obvious to her that she was being rewarded, and to refuse would have hurt their feelings. And, upon reflection, a day in town would be nice—she had her pay-packet almost untouched and there were things she needed.

She spent Sunday tidying her room, sitting in the yard with Charles and going for a long, rambling walk in the afternoon. There was a cottage outside

136

the village where teas were to be got; she had hers there, bought two pasties from the obliging owner and had her supper in her room with Charles for company. Since Knott was leaving in the morning, she went to bed betimes.

She wore the rose-printed dress and the new shoes and even Mrs Legge, who praised seldom, admitted that she looked quite the lady.

'Well, she is, isn't she?' observed Parsons forthrightly, watching from the kitchen window as Sarah got into the car beside Knott. 'And not all the caps and aprons in the world can make her anything else.' When Mrs Legge grudgingly agreed, she said, 'I'll go over and make sure that Charles of hers is all right. Dotes on the beast, she does. Seems she hadn't got anything or anyone else to dote on, more's the pity.'

It was a splendid morning and London, when they reached it an hour later, looked inviting. Knott set her down at Piccadilly Circus, arranged to pick her up at six o'clock outside the tube station there and drove off. Sarah stood for a minute deciding what to do first. It was still early—perhaps it would be sensible to make her small purchases first, and then be free to window-shop or walk in one of the parks. Half an hour later, her shopping done, she walked slowly up Regent Street. Half an hour in Liberty's would be pleasant before she found a small café for coffee. The half-hour stretched into an hour or more; she came out into Regent Street at length and stood on the kerb, ready to nip across the street when there was a gap in the traffic.

There was a smartly dressed woman hoping to do the same thing, standing beside her. She looked

sideways at Sarah and grinned. 'Give me New York
any time,' she observed. 'What wouldn't I give for
wings...'

She paused as a Rolls-Royce came to a smooth
stop at the kerb's edge. The door was opened and
the Professor said, 'Get in, Sarah.'

Sarah swallowed back her heart. 'I don't
want——' she began.

Wasted breath. 'Get in,' said the Professor again,
this time with a note in his voice which she did not
care to ignore; besides, the girl from New York
chimed in, 'Get in, Sarah, do! You must be nuts...'
She gave Sarah a little push and, after a quick look
at the Professor's unsmiling face, Sarah got in.

But she didn't give up easily, 'I don't want——'
she began once more and was halted by his, 'Later,
later, we can't argue in the middle of Regent Street.'
So she subsided, mulling over all the things she intended to say to him when she had the chance.
When would that be? she wondered. The traffic was
mostly one way, and he turned into Haymarket,
back into lower Regent Street and then into St
James's Street, passed Berkeley Square and on
towards Cavendish Square, but he turned off into
one of the narrow streets on either side and stopped
halfway down a short quiet street lined with
Georgian town houses.

'Where is this?' asked Sarah in a rather high
voice.

The Professor got out, walked round the car to
open her door and said, 'I live here.' He smiled
down at her and her heart rocked. 'I hope you will
give me the pleasure of lunching with me.'

She got out of the car and stared up at him. 'No, oh, no, I don't think so, thank you all the same. There is no need. I was only going to cross the road, you know,' she added wildly, 'but you stopped.'

His voice was kind. 'We are so often at odds, aren't we? Perhaps we could forget our personal feelings just for an hour or two and have lunch together.' He smiled again. 'It was my clinic this morning, I thought it would never end. I should like to talk about something other than cerebral catastrophes and diabetes. You shall sit at my table, Sarah, and let me ramble on and you, being you, will give the right answers at the right moment so that I shall be soothed into good humour once more and face my afternoon patients with sympathy and patience.'

She listened to this speech in some astonishment. 'Is that why you stopped?' she asked.

He uttered the lie blandly. 'Of course, why else?' He eyed her narrowly. 'I suppose in my present mood anyone would have done.'

It was on the tip of her tongue to tell him that in that case he could hunt around for someone else, but she was a kind girl—moreover, she loved him. She said rather primly, 'Very well, I will have lunch with you, Professor, but I still have some shopping to do,' which was a fib.

'I shall be delighted to drive you back to wherever you want to go,' he assured her gravely. 'Shall we go indoors?'

Brindle opened the door; he had been standing discreetly in the hall watching them with great interest through the side window. Here was a little tit-bit of news for Mrs Brindle presently, he reflected, as he closed the door, took his master's briefcase and Sarah's plastic shopping bag and opened the drawing-room door.

'This is Brindle,' said the Professor. 'He and his wife look after me very well. Brindle, this is Miss Fletcher, who will be lunching with me. Would you ask Mrs Brindle to show her where she can tidy herself?'

Sarah was led away by a tall, bony woman with a friendly face, to be shown into a cloakroom beside the gracefully curved staircase. It had everything needful for the refurbishing of one's person, but before she started to comb her hair into perfect smoothness she stood peering at her face in the long looking-glass. After a moment she sighed and started on her hair. There was no way in which her unassuming features could be transformed into beauty; besides, she reminded herself soberly, she was twenty-eight.

She could hear a dog barking as she went back into the hall, and a door opened and Trotter came prancing to meet her. She stooped to hug her and the Professor followed the dog in. 'Come and have a drink,' he invited, and held the door wide open. The room was large, with windows at both ends and a wide fireplace facing the door, flanked by two sofas with a low table between. There were easy-chairs, too, upholstered in tapestry, and the tall windows were elaborately draped in claret-coloured satin. The floor was beeswaxed and was covered almost entirely by a Persian carpet, whose faded colours echoed the shade of the curtains. There were flowers, too, great bowls of roses and sweet-smelling stocks. It would be a lovely room at night, reflected

Sarah, sitting down at one end of a sofa. There were lamps all over the place, shaded in a soft mushroom-pink. A room to be happy in, she decided. The Professor might prefer his home at Minster Lovell, but he must surely be content with his London home too.

'Sherry?' he asked, and handed her a glass before sitting down opposite her, but a little to one side so that he could watch her face from his armchair.

It amused him to see her obviously struggling to find something to say, and when after a few moments she ventured, 'It's quiet here, not like London at all,' he smiled gently and began to talk easily so that presently she lost her shyness and, by the time they crossed the hall to the dining-room, they were engrossed in a lively discussion about pruning roses, a subject which led to a variety of other topics while they ate their iced melon, jellied chicken with a green salad and finally strawberries and *fromage blanc*. They had drunk a white burgundy with their meal and Sarah, so much put at her ease that she quite forgot her circumstances, said, 'Oh, Puligny-Montrachet—how very nice . . .'

The Professor sat back in his chair, his eyes gleaming. 'You know something about wines, Sarah?'

She blushed finely at that. 'No, oh, no, only my father—years ago—used to tell me about them, and—and I just happened to remember this one.' She added very ingenuously, 'Was I rude?'

He let out a crack of laughter. 'My dear Sarah, of course not. I suspect that you are hiding your light under a bushel, though. Tell me, do you not find it difficult at times at Lady Wesley's?'

'Difficult? You mean the work? It's only housework, you know, and we each have our own jobs to do——'

'I meant your—er—colleagues in the kitchen.'

'They're splendid,' she declared warmly. 'Kind and generous, and if I do something wrong they put me right without scolding. They're friends.'

'You have no wish to change your job?' He spoke casually and, her tongue nicely loosened, she answered readily, although she didn't look at him.

'I have a home, somewhere where Charles can live too, and work to keep me busy. I can save, too, and I'm not lonely.' She ended on a defiant note but he didn't dispute the last point, even though he didn't believe her.

'You would not wish to marry?' His voice was quiet, inviting her confidence.

She looked at him with eyes as clear as a child's. 'Of course I'd like to marry. I'm twenty-eight, you know that, Professor, and I have no looks to speak of. I don't meet many people and I have no—no background. It seems to me that it is unlikely that I shall marry, don't you agree? It's no good crying for the moon.'

'Some day, Sarah, someone will come along and give you the moon, and the stars too.'

She shook her head, managing to smile, and said lightly, 'I'll believe that when it happens.'

'If I were to tell you——' began the Professor, but was interrupted by the phone ringing and Brindle going to answer it.

'Miss Lisse, sir,' he announced, 'wishful to speak to you.'

The Professor got up. 'Excuse me a moment, Sarah,' he said and went into the hall, leaving the door wide open, so that Sarah, even if she hadn't wanted to, couldn't help but hear every word he uttered.

Who was Lisse? she wondered, and strained her ears to hear better.

The Professor sounded pleased and his voice was warm, quite unlike his usual detached calm. 'Darling,' she heard him say, 'this is a lovely surprise, where are you?' There was a pause, then, 'No, I'll come and fetch you and bring you here. We must have time to talk about the wedding.' There was another pause, a long one which gave Sarah time to pull herself together. After all, why should she feel all at once broken-hearted? The Professor had never even looked at her, and anyone with any sense would know that a man such as he wouldn't remain a bachelor forever. She had known that loving him was hopeless—more, ludicrous, and she had got what she deserved. Listeners never heard any good of themselves.

He came back to the table presently and began to talk about the garden at Minster Lovell while they drank their coffee, and when they had finished and gone back to the drawing-room, Sarah observed in her calm voice that she still had some shopping to do and felt that she should be going. 'Knott is picking me up,' she explained, 'and I don't want to keep him waiting.'

The Professor made no effort to keep her. 'I've a visit to make before my afternoon patients,' he told her. 'I'll drop you off.' And when she thanked him without fuss, he said, 'I have enjoyed our lunch. Thank you for keeping me company, Sarah.'

'Lunch was delightful,' she told him gravely. 'Thank you for inviting me.'

She wished Brindle goodbye, followed the Professor out to his car and got in beside him. She sat silent while he drove through the pleasant streets in the direction of Oxford Street.

'Anywhere in particular?' he asked, and wondered why she was so pale and silent; and, when she said, 'Anywhere in Oxford Street or Regent Street, thank you,' dismissed the thought.

He stopped in a narrow road running into Regent Street and got out. He opened her door and said, 'I'm sorry I can't stop in Regent Street, but will this do, it's only a step——?'

'It will do very well, and thank you again, Professor.'

He put a hand on her arm as she stood beside him. 'Tell me, Sarah, do you always think of me as Professor?'

She met his eye and smiled a little. 'Not always. Thank you again and goodbye, Professor.'

He got back into the car and watched her small person until it disappeared round the corner into Regent Street, then he drove on.

Sarah filled in the remaining hours of the afternoon with lengthy inspections of Marks and Spencer and British Home Stores. She would far rather have looked in the boutiques in Bond Street and the Burlington Arcade, but there was no point in drooling over clothes she couldn't have. She bought a bottle of wine, and after a cup of tea made her way through the crowds to Picadilly Tube Station.

She had judged the time nicely, and she hadn't been waiting for more than five minutes when Knott drew up. He leaned over to open the door and she jumped in, fastened her seatbelt and answered him cheerfully when he enquired about her day. And when she said that yes, she had enjoyed it, he said gloomily that that was more than he had done. 'Hanging around waiting for people to give me letters and delivering parcels. Can't think why her ladyship doesn't use the post.'

'Well,' said Sarah reasonably, 'they could all have been important, and she needed someone trustworthy to collect and deliver them.'

Knott looked smugly pleased with himself. 'Well, perhaps you're right,' he conceded. 'Been with the family most of my life.'

'Well, there, that's it then, Mr Knott.'

They talked comfortably as he drove back to Lady Wesley's house, set her down at the side door and drove on to the garage. Sarah went to her cottage, made much of Charles, fed him and let him out, and tidied herself before going along to the kitchen for her supper. Mr Cork was there, reading the paper, and she gave him the bottle of wine. 'You have all been so kind and helped me so much,' she told him diffidently. 'I hope you won't think it presumptuous of me, I don't mean to be, I just want to say thank you...'

Cork looked surprised; housemaids, in his experience, didn't buy bottles of wine—and very superior wine too, he noticed as he took the bottle—and offer them to the butler. But Fletcher wasn't quite a normal housemaid—she was always polite, quick to do as she was asked by her domestic betters, but on the other hand not in the least in awe of them.

He said, rather pompously, 'Why, Fletcher, this is most kind of you. I'm sure we shall all enjoy a glass with our supper. A nice thought, and much appreciated.'

As he said to Mrs Legge later that evening, he hadn't the heart to snub Sarah. 'She does a housemaid's work as well as any girl I've had under me, but she's not the type, if you see what I mean.' And Mrs Legge saw.

It was several days later, as they sat round the kitchen table drinking their mid-morning cup of tea, that Miss Mudd joined them. Normally she considered herself above elevenses, but now she sat down, accepted a cup of tea and looked around her, obviously full of news.

It was Mrs Legge who asked her if anything untoward had happened.

Miss Mudd sipped her tea daintily and looked around the table. 'I was in her ladyship's dressing-room, and when the phone rang I answered it as I always do. It was Professor Nauta, so I took her the phone and went back to the dressing-room. The door was open and her ladyship has a very clear voice. Not,' she added primly, 'that I would stoop to eavesdropping, but I couldn't help but overhear. Splendid news, she says, all excited like, and when is the wedding to be, Radolf? And she listens a bit and says, such a sweet girl, you must be very happy, and then she says, it will be a big affair, I suppose, and she listened a bit more. Well, it is the bride's day, you'll have to put up with that, she says, and listens a bit more...' Miss Mudd hesitated. 'She told me to shut the door then, but not before I heard her say, your mother will be over the moon.'

She sat back, satisfied with the interest she had stirred in her listeners. There were murmurs of 'A wedding, eh?' 'And such a handsome man he is, too,' and Mr Cork's considered observation that he had always said that the Professor had it in mind to marry. In the general flurry of conversation Sarah's pale face went unnoticed, as did her silence. Only later that day Mrs Legge observed to Cook that Fletcher looked a bit peaky. 'And I can't say I'm surprised,' she added, 'for she did more than her share of work today—didn't stop once, and offered to polish the silver for Parsons when she said she had a headache.'

The day to Sarah seemed endless. When she at last got to her cottage, she fed Charles and went into the yard with him. There was no one about and the evening was fine and warm, and so she sat there while he pottered about and when, at length, she was in bed, with him curled up at her feet, she allowed herself to think. It wasn't a surprise, after all, she reminded herself; she had known about Lisse, and she had no reason to feel as though the bottom of her world had fallen out. Just the same, she told an unresponsive Charles, she hoped that she would never see the Professor again.

He came to lunch the next day, and instead of ringing the bell beside the front door, as any caller should, he chose to stroll round the house to the garage. He had someone with him and they both came to a halt at the sight of Sarah, armed with the impedimenta for the cleaning of windows, tying a sacking apron over her cotton dress.

They were close enough for her to hear the Professor's testy, 'What in the name of the Almighty do you think you're doing, Sarah?'

She turned smartly, but before she could say a word, he said, 'And hold your tongue about my language.'

It was his companion who broke a silence pregnant with ill temper. 'Good Lord, Sarah— fancy seeing you here.' He examined her appearance in a puzzled way. 'Are you doing something for a bet, or is it one of those charity things? I heard you were in London.'

Sarah eyed him without pleasure. He was all she needed to spoil a day already made wretched by the Professor's appearance. She said crossly, 'Oh, hello, Wilfred. Well, I was in London, but now I'm here and don't you dare tell a soul.'

'You know each other?' asked the Professor blandly. 'So nice to meet old friends.'

The young man turned a pleasant, eager face to him. 'Yes, sir. We've known each other for years. Lived in the same village. Bit of a shock meeting Sarah here, especially dressed like a kitchen maid.'

'I am the housemaid,' said Sarah tartly, 'and what are you doing here, anyway?'

'Still snappy, Sarah,' he remarked cheerfully. 'Always ready to take a chap down a peg or two. Didn't know I'd managed to pass my exams, did you? I'm Professor Nauta's houseman.'

'Congratulations,' said Sarah.

The Professor gave a small cough. 'Er—Fitzgibbon, I believe we should leave Sarah to finish her work.'

Wilfred said hastily, 'Oh, of course, sir.' He darted another puzzled look at Sarah. 'I'll give you a ring,' he suggested.

'Don't you dare, Wilf. You can write, but don't expect an answer.'

The two men strolled away, and nothing in the Professor's appearance of detached amusement betrayed his overpowering wish to hurl Sarah's bucket and brushes into the bushes, tear off that deplorable sacking apron and carry her off to some remote spot, where, he reflected savagely, he would have the greatest pleasure in wringing her small neck—but first of all he would elicit from her the exact nature of her friendship with young Fitzgibbon. They had known each other all their lives, and there was an easy familiarity between them. He frowned so ferociously that young Fitzgibbon, about to embark on some harmless observation, thought it prudent to remain silent.

Sarah finished her windows, emptied the bucket and went back to the house. Mr Cork was waiting for her. 'Fletcher, leave those things, Molly will see to them. Go to your room and change into your afternoon uniform. Parsons has cut her hand and will be unable to serve lunch, so you must do it for her. Now hurry, you have no more than ten minutes or so.'

Sarah so far forgot herself as to ask, 'Must I, Mr Cork? I don't——'

He stopped her with a majestic movement of a hand and an outraged look from his prominent eyes. 'You will do as you are told, my girl, and look smart about it.'

So Sarah tore over to her cottage, gave Charles his dinner, flung off her cotton dress and got into the black one, tied a clean white afternoon apron about her person, washed her face and hands rather sketchily, combed her hair into a semblance of tidiness, pinned on her cap and tore back again just in time to take up her station by the sideboard. She had the greatest difficulty in not giggling when Lady Wesley came in with her two guests—the Professor looked furious and Wilfred completely bewildered.

Under Cork's critical eye she handed out soup, offered sole, spinach and new potatoes, removed plates and, when she wasn't doing that, stood like a black and white statue, looking into the middle distance. Rather difficult, since the Professor was sitting exactly opposite to where she was standing.

In order to take her mind off him, she concentrated on the conversation. From it she gleaned the information that Wilfred's mother had been a schoolfriend of Lady Wesley, and through her had met Mevrouw Nauta, who naturally enough had told her son, hence his invitation to take his houseman to meet Lady Wesley. She would have to get hold of Wilf before they left and get him to promise not to say a word about her to anyone . . . She nipped smartly to the table once more, took plates away and offered cream for the trifle Lady Wesley was dispensing, while Cork solemnly poured wine.

Coffee was to be served in the drawing-room, a task which Cork undertook leaving Sarah to clear the table and go back to the kitchen, where she sat down beside the injured Parsons and ate a splendid meal of steak and kidney pie with spotted dick to follow. Mrs Legge, a stern taskmistress, was nevertheless generous when it came to feeding the staff. And she was fair, too—when the meal was finished she told Sarah that she might go at once to her cottage since she had taken over Parsons' work at a moment's notice. 'But please be back at half-past four, Fletcher. Parsons can get the tea laid up, but you had better take it in. Lady Wesley will object to Parsons' bandaged hand.'

There were more than two hours before half-past four. Sarah got into a cotton dress, brushed her hair and tied it back, opened her door and went into the yard with Charles. It was warm and quiet. She sat doing nothing for quite some time and then, remembering that she must try and see Wilfred if possible, she took Charles indoors and went out again. As long as they kept in the background, Lady Wesley had no objection to the staff walking in the grounds. Sarah began a circuit of the house, keeping well away from it, hoping that Wilfred might possibly be wandering about on his own while Lady Wesley and the Professor talked. Not that it was likely, she reflected bitterly; Wilf had never been noted for tact. There was no sign of anyone, and she made her way to the garage in the forlorn hope that he might be there. And he was, standing beside the Rolls deep in admiration.

'There you are,' said Sarah crossly. 'I must talk to you for a moment. You're to promise not to breathe a word to anyone about me, and I mean anyone—you know how people talk.' She smiled suddenly at him. 'Wilf, dear, do please promise. I know you think I'm out of my mind, but I'm really quite happy here. It's so nice after London, almost like home...' She paused a moment and then went on steadily, 'Promise?'

He looked worried. 'Well, I suppose I must, but isn't there something else you could do, Sarah? I know you don't want to go home, we all know how your stepmother treated you after your father died, but couldn't you be in an office or something more—more suitable?'

'I was in an office and I lived in a beastly little room in a dreary street and I had no friends at all. But here I have a tiny cottage all to myself and the staff are so kind and they are my friends and on my day off there's country all around. Oh, Wilf, you must understand.'

He said reluctantly, 'Oh, well, all right, I promise.'

She flung her arms round his neck and kissed him, and the Professor, chatting with Knott and an interested spectator had, for the second time that day, a violent urge to wring Sarah's neck. A good thing that Knott was standing with his back to them and hadn't seen any of it, he thought, listening with apparent deep interest to Knott's opinion of lead-free petrol.

Promptly at half-past four, Sarah followed Mr Cork into the drawing-room carrying the cake stand, a lace tablecloth and tea plates. Lady Wesley was old-fashioned; tea, for her, was an elegant little meal with paper-thin sandwiches, tiny cakes and, when her guests were men, one of Cook's Madeira cakes. Sarah arranged everything just so, and, while Cork stood at the door, handed out the teacups as

Lady Wesley poured the tea. That done to her satisfaction, Lady Wesley sat back comfortably. 'Thank you, Cork,' she said, 'and you can go, Fletcher. I'll ring if I need more hot water.'

'Very good, La—my lady,' said Sarah, remembering just in time, and she slid away, taking a look at the Professor as she went. The coldness of his eyes fastened on her sent a nasty shiver down her back.

She went down to the kitchen and had her tea, and began to collect the silver and glass ready for Parsons to set the table under Mr Cork's eagle eye. Lady Wesley would be dining alone. 'So you can have half an hour to yourself, Sarah,' said Mrs Legge. 'Be here at six o'clock to lay our supper.'

Sarah escaped thankfully, but she didn't get far. Cork's voice stopped her as she was crossing to her cottage. 'Professor Nauta wishes to speak to you, Fletcher. He has messages from Mevrouw Nauta. He is in the hall—don't keep him waiting.'

So Sarah went reluctantly back again and found the Professor standing by the door, his hand on the latch. He opened it when he saw her and waved her through into the garden beyond, and, when she would have stood there in the porch, said impatiently, 'Not here, we'll go through the shrubbery.'

'What was the message?' asked Sarah, trotting to keep up. 'I'm free for half an hour and I want to feed Charles. I mean, we don't have to walk miles, do we? Is it important?'

He stopped and stood looking down at her. 'I have no idea, for I have no message. But I wished to speak to you, and I needed a reason which wouldn't raise eyebrows and at the same time make it impossible for you to ignore my request.'

She stared at his tie, trying to gather the right words. 'I am not sure why I annoy you so much,' she said at length, 'but you don't have to feel responsible for me just because I lost my job at St Cyprian's, and I'm quite content here, really I am.'

'Tell me, Sarah, young Fitzgibbon, are you fond of each other?'

Here was the opening she had been looking for. If she said yes, then the Professor would feel free to go and forget her. 'Oh, very,' she said. She went on chattily, 'I thought I'd never see him again, but now everything will be all right. Once he gets started with a practice of his own...' She left the rest of the sentence hanging speculatively in mid-air.

'You will marry?' The Professor's voice was nicely casual.

In for a penny, in for a pound, reflected Sarah, and she said, 'Oh, yes, of course. So you see, you don't have to bother... you can forget me with a clear conscience.'

When he didn't say anything, she said, 'What was it you wanted to say to me, Professor?'

'Nothing of any importance.' He sounded detached, almost bored. 'As you say, I need no longer concern myself with you.'

They turned and began to walk back towards the house with nothing further to say, which was a good thing, for Sarah's voice was drowned in tears which she would die rather than shed. At the door he said briskly, 'Young Fitzgibbon will be wondering where I have got to. Goodbye, Sarah.'

If she said anything, she would burst into tears. She nodded in his general direction and fled indoors.

The Professor made no effort to rejoin Wilfred, but stood where she had left him, going over their conversation. It hadn't been the one he had intended, and despite Sarah's remarks about her future they hadn't rung quite true in his ears. He had wished her goodbye, but he had no intention of keeping to that. Now he knew where she was it would be easy enough to keep an eye on her. He strolled towards the garage where Wilfred was waiting for him. Sarah had somehow wormed her way into his orderly life, and he found it disquieting that she was a perpetual worry to him. What was more, he didn't consider young Fitzgibbon a suitable husband for her. He waited for the feeling of relief her news should have engendered in him, and felt merely a rising sense of annoyance.

'I have never met such a tiresome girl,' he muttered as he came in sight of the patient Wilfred.

Driving back to London, he edged the talk round to the subject of Sarah. 'Quite some surprise for you meeting her like that,' he observed casually. 'You must have been delighted to see her again.'

Wilfred, anxious to please, made the reply he thought was expected of him. 'Oh, rather, sir. Though I must say I was a bit put out to see her working like that. I mean, it just isn't her scene. Mind you, she could turn her hand to most things and is splendid at running a house and so on. She did it all when her father was alive—before he married again, that is.'

The Professor murmured encouragingly and Wilfred went on, glad to have something to talk about with this man, who, although he wouldn't admit it even to himself, rather intimidated him. 'She'll make a splendid wife.' He didn't see the Professor's quick frown. 'Just the kind of girl to encourage a man on his way up the ladder. Oh, well, I don't suppose it will be long before she leaves that job and settles down.' He felt a rush of brotherly affection for Sarah. 'I shall do my best to persuade her,' he declared largely.

The Professor had thought that Sarah might have been exaggerating, but now he had heard her story corroborated, something which should on the face of things have pleased him. But he felt no pleasure, only a mounting feeling of annoyance that her future appeared to be settled without any help from him.

He dropped Wilfred off at the hospital with the remark that he would see him in the morning, and drove himself home where he brooded over his dinner, was terse with Brindle and sat up far too late with Trotter for company. He was an abstemious man, but he had drunk rather too much whisky before he went at last to his bed.

CHAPTER EIGHT

SARAH settled down to the rather monotonous round of her day's work. She had made up her mind to be sensible—brooding over something she could never have wouldn't help at all. She resolved not to think about the Professor at all, but despite this he was there, inside her head for all her waking hours, and if she dreamed, it was of him. Nevertheless, she persevered, and on her day off, if it fell on a weekday, she took herself off to Bedford. There were some good shops there, and she began to spend some, at least, of her money, laying it out carefully, replenishing a wardrobe which was woefully scanty. After her shopping she took herself off to a restaurant and had lunch. It was lonely, but she had become used to that over the years.

Of the Professor there was no sign, and she told herself that that was a good thing. Out of sight, out of mind, she reminded herself over and over again and, so that she wouldn't have time to sit and think, she worked rather harder than she needed to. She became a little thin and seemed pale, despite the lovely weather, but there was nothing wrong with her work. Cork, discussing her with Mrs Legge, gave it as his opinion that despite her cheerful appearance she was unhappy. 'Not the kind of young woman to show it, Mrs Legge,' he stated, 'nor the kind of young woman to be asked what is up, if you see what I mean.' He drank the tea Mrs

Legge offered him. 'Of course, this isn't her accompaniment.'

Mrs Legge, who wasn't quite sure what accompaniment meant, nodded her head wisely. 'Indeed not, Mr Cork. You are a very discerning man, if I may say so.'

The Professor, when he arrived to take lunch with his Aunt Beatrice on the following day, proved to be just as discerning. One brief look at Sarah's face allowed him to see that something was wrong. He had noted with approval on his previous visits that her small person had achieved a pleasing plumpness and that her pale London face had become healthy and pink, but now the pink had faded and she had become thin. She was probably hankering after young Fitzgibbon, in which case he supposed he would have to take a hand in their affairs. There were flats around the hospital where the married doctors could live. No doubt he could arrange things so that the next one to come empty should go to the boy, and he and Sarah could marry. In that event, he himself would be able to keep an eye on her. The Professor, no longer in a state to order his thoughts, found nothing strange in this idea. Before he went back to London, he would contrive to have a word with her. He had seen her only briefly when he had arrived, and it was Parsons who served lunch with Cork, but an opportunity would have to be made.

As it turned out, the opportunity presented itself without any effort on his part. As they sat chatting by the open doors of the drawing-room after lunch, Lady Wesley said, 'While you are here, Radolf, would you take a look at Fletcher? Mrs Legge tells

me that she is getting rather thin, and although she
works very hard and gives every satisfaction, she
remains pale and quiet. Possibly she is anaemic and
needs a tonic?'

Never having suffered anything more serious than
a heavy cold in the head, Lady Wesley was out of
date regarding medical matters. 'A tonic?' she
repeated. 'My mother always kept a bottle of tonic
for the servants.'

The Professor looked at his relation with mild
affection and well-concealed amusement. Like so
many comfortably placed people, while not stinting
herself in any way, if it was possible to get something for nothing, she did so. His fees, if he cared
to remind her, would probably give her a mild heart
attack.

'Yes, of course I'll see her.' He glanced at his
watch. 'I shall have to leave in about half an hour,
so how about my taking a look at her now? You
have your nap, don't you? I'll say goodbye and not
disturb you when I leave. If there is anything
seriously amiss I will let Mrs Legge know.'

'Thank you, Radolf. If you wouldn't mind going
to Mrs Legge's room? I'll send for Fletcher to go
there.'

So Sarah, sitting in the yard with Charles enjoying the sun and half-asleep, was summoned to
go to Mrs Legge's room and to look sharp about
it. Since Parsons, who had been given the task of
fetching her, had no idea why she was wanted, she
was quite unprepared for the sight of the Professor
engaged in conversation with the housekeeper.

Mrs Legge addressed her in a no-nonsense voice.
'Her ladyship has asked Professor Nauta to see you,

Fletcher. I have been uneasy about you for the last week or so. You are not quite yourself, perhaps a tonic... The Professor will decide that.' She glanced at him. 'You said that you preferred to see Sarah alone, sir. I shall be in the servants' hall if you should need me.'

The Professor opened the door for her, closed it gently behind her and stood leaning against it, looking at Sarah. 'Let me set your mind at rest,' he begged silkily. 'My godmother cannot resist getting something for nothing, and since I am here and a doctor, she seized the opportunity to secure my services for free. I do not think that she is in the least worried about your health, but Mrs Legge and Cork certainly are. Sit down and tell me what is wrong, Sarah, and remember that we are patient and doctor and nothing more.'

She sat, and was glad to do so for her legs felt like jelly, but his explanation had given her time to pull herself together and she said quietly, 'But I am not ill, Professor, indeed I am not...'

'Then there is something worrying you?' His voice was kind now, and gentle. 'Trouble with your stepmother, perhaps?' When she shook her head he said, after a pause, 'But you are unhappy; do you know, you remind me of *Twelfth Night*— "With a green and yellow melancholy, she sat like patience on a monument, smiling at grief."' And, when she looked at him, 'She never told her love, did she? And I suspect you are in like case, Sarah?'

He watched the colour flood over her pale face and sighed. Really, she was twenty-eight and surely old enough to sort out her own love life. She was sitting there looking not a day older than eighteen.

He supposed that she and young Fitzgibbon had quarrelled—he would discover that easily enough, since Wilfred tended to look upon him as a god-like father confessor.

He said, 'Lady Wesley and Mrs Legge are of the opinion that you should be given a tonic. I cannot remember ever prescribing one, but since it is expected of me I shall write you up for a glass of Guinness with your dinner.'

'I don't like it,' said Sarah in a positive voice.

'Nevertheless you will drink it, Sarah, and I will reassure Mrs Legge that you haven't fallen into a decline, and that you will recover your normal good spirits very shortly.' He said, suddenly harsh, 'And for heaven's sake, let this be the last time we meet.'

She got up slowly. She had never felt so unhappy in her life before. She wanted to turn and run—to the other side of the world, as far away from her unhappiness as possible, only she couldn't do that. She felt numb and unable to think, let alone say anything. And what was there to say? Radolf didn't want to see her ever again, and that made sense. He was going to be married shortly and her heart would break. People laughed at broken hearts... She didn't look at him or speak, but opened the door and walked away on legs which didn't seem to belong to her any more.

As for the Professor, he spent five minutes with Mrs Legge and then got into his car and drove himself back to London, in a thoroughly bad temper.

It was perhaps fortunate for his registrar and housemen that he was leaving on a short lecture tour the following day. It would take him to

Birmingham, Edinburgh and Aberdeen, and when
he returned he was flying out to the Middle East
to join a consultation of learned gentlemen con-
cerning the health of an oil magnate. Brindle,
packing his bag for him, gave it as his opinion that
a week or two in different surroundings would
benefit everyone as well as the Professor, and Mrs
Brindle, eyeing the tasty meal returned to the
kitchen half-eaten, agreed with him.

Sarah drank her Guinness with her dinner, but
it was evident that it wasn't doing her much good.
She became a little thinner and paler, even though
she remained as cheerful as she always had been.

'It is my opinion,' said Miss Mudd, drinking a
genteel cup of tea with Mrs Legge, 'that the girl is
in love.'

'Such a quiet, plain little thing, too, but not
lacking in backbone.'

The two ladies nodded wisely to each other.

Sarah, unaware of their concern, did her work
and got through her days as best she could. She
supposed that given time she would get over the
Professor, consign him to the very back of her mind
and eventually forget him entirely, although just at
the moment that seemed to be an impossibility.

The Professor returned, outwardly at least his
usual coldly polite self, and, since he had a backlog
of patients to deal with at the hospital as well as a
formidable list of private patients to work his way
through, he saw little of young Fitzgibbon out of
working hours. He had been back a week or more
before he found himself with ten minutes to spare
and his young houseman with him.

'Any plans to get married yet?' he asked casually.

Wilfred beamed at him. 'Well, sir, we would like to—I mean, we've settled our differences finally and of course we'll have to find somewhere to live. She wanted to go on working, but of course I can't allow that. Janet thinks I'm old-fashioned——'

'Janet?' queried the Professor sharply.

'That's her name, sir. Janet Burrows—she's a staff nurse on the surgical side. We've known each other for a couple of years, and we've been waiting until I got started.'

The look of mild interest on the Professor's face didn't waver, while he sternly suppressed surprised delight and at the same time rage against Sarah. He said, still casually, 'Well, you are started now, aren't you? I believe that Dr Wilkinson is leaving in a couple of months. If you would like it, I think I could put in a good word for you.'

Wilfred went scarlet with emotion. 'Sir, could you really? I say, that would be splendid. We could get married——'

'That was the idea,' said the Professor mildly. 'You have eight or nine months still to work here, haven't you? Take my advice and try for a junior registrar's post in a smallish hospital. By the end of another year you should be capable of a GP's job at a health centre.'

'I say, sir, you are good. My word, wait until Janet hears this.'

The Professor glanced at his watch. 'I can dispense with your services for half an hour. Be in Men's Medical at half-past five.' He nodded and stalked away, and Wilfred took himself over to the surgical wing to find his Janet.

As for the Professor, he went along to his consulting-room at his clinic, shut the door and straight away sat down to think. He had a lot to think about, and his thoughts were wholly of Sarah. They were interrupted by the return of Wilfred, cock-a-hoop and bursting with gratitude, and the Professor gave up his daydreams for the moment and bent his sapient mind to the problems facing him in Men's Medical.

He returned home that evening, and Brindle took one look at his face and at once confided in Mrs Brindle that whatever it was that had been upsetting the Professor had been dealt with satisfactorily, an opinion which was corroborated when he demolished the excellent dinner she had cooked for him and then took himself down to the kitchen to compliment her on it.

'Well, I never did,' she told Brindle. 'It can't be his job, for he can't go no higher, surely to goodness. He's in love.'

They exchanged the kind of glance married couples exchange. 'That nice young lady who came to lunch,' said Mrs Brindle, and smiled and nodded.

As for the Professor, he and Trotter went into his study where Trotter went instantly to sleep, and he dealt with the papers on his desk. Only then did he sit back and allow his thoughts to wander. He tried to remember how he had felt about Sarah when she had been working at the clinic, and came to the rueful conclusion that he hadn't felt anything at all. She had been the quiet, rather plain girl, with a surprisingly sharp tongue if she was put out, lovely eyes and pretty hair and a way of looking very directly at one . . .

Now he had to admit that she had become more important to him than anyone else in the world. The idea of a future without her wasn't to be borne. She had by some mysterious metamorphosis become more beautiful than anyone else he had ever encountered.

'How do you like the idea?' he asked Trotter, and stirred the dog gently with his foot. Trotter opened an eye, rumbled gently and closed it again. 'You'll have to share her with Charles,' the Professor reminded him.

Sarah, unaware of the future the Professor was planning for her, went to bed each evening and wept quietly into Charles' comforting fur, and each morning got up with the stern resolve not to think any more about him. An easy resolve to keep, as it happened, for Lady Wesley had invited guests for the weekend and was planning a party for her birthday. When Sarah heard about it, she plucked up the courage to ask Cork if she need go into the dining-room. 'I almost let you down,' she reminded him, 'that time I nearly dropped the cheese. I suppose it's the smell of the food that makes me feel giddy, Mr Cork.'

Certainly, clumsiness at the dining table wouldn't do at all, Mr Cork agreed. As it happened, Mrs Willis was asking him only the other day if there was any casual work for her. 'Cook can do with extra help in the kitchen, since there will be eighteen for dinner.' He frowned importantly. 'I will grant your request, Fletcher, for there is sense in it. A mishap at table would not do. But you will have to help serve this weekend. There are only three guests: Colonel and Mrs Phelps and the Honourable Miss

Bennett.' He gave Sarah a severe look. 'And see that you do your work well, Fletcher.'

She thanked him, and went back to her vacuuming very relieved. The Professor would certainly be one of the guests at the birthday party, but if she was in the kitchen there would be no chance of encountering him. The weekend, made busy by the three elderly and somewhat demanding guests, passed uneventfully, and the household set about getting ready for the birthday party. There was to be a dinner for eighteen persons first, and then some forty or fifty guests for the evening. Sarah was very busy, running to and fro, fetching flowers for Miss Mudd who fancied herself as a disciple of Constance Spry, descending to the cellar to help Cork bring up the wines, pleasantly giving Cook a hand and polishing silver and glass. The caterers would deal with the evening's entertainment, but Cook had every intention of excelling herself with the dinner. There was furniture to move, the dining table to lengthen, sufficient linen to be brought down from the vast linen cupboard on the second floor and, since Sarah was quick on her feet and willing, it fell to her lot to trot up and down with whatever Mrs Legge selected.

She was tired at the end of her day, but she welcomed that, for she had no time to think about the Professor—although she was aware that his image was firmly implanted at the back of her head and would never go away.

The summer weather was exceptional, and Lady Wesley's birthday dawned clear and sunny. Sarah, up early like everyone else in the house and on the run all day, was ready for her bed as the first of the guests arrived. The kitchen was uncomfortably warm, but at least it was a safe hiding-place.

Parsons, nipping down for a quick cup of tea before the gong sounded, reported the ladies' dresses, their hairstyles and any gossip she had overheard. 'That Miss de Foe-Burgess is here, wearing red crêpe—all wrong for her—and rolling her eyes at all the men. Professor Nauta's here too, looking ever so pleased with himself.' She swallowed the rest of her tea and darted away again as the gong sounded and Sarah, under Cook's watchful eye, began to put the dishes in the food-lift. The dinner was a success, reported Cork, and he told Sarah to go up to the dining-room and clear the table. 'Parsons is up there, and there's more than enough work for one.'

So Sarah slid upstairs, looking carefully in all directions in case the Professor was lurking in a corner. But he wasn't. She gained the dining-room, helped Parsons and then, mindful of Mr Cork's instructions nipped smartly across the back of the hall to the service door. The sight of a housemaid in a print dress and rather dishevelled as well would shock the guests, he had cautioned her. She gained the door and slid through, giving a last look round the hall as she did so. The Professor was at the other end of the hall, watching her. Too far away to see his expression, she felt an urge to run to him so great that she very nearly did just that. She whisked herself to her side of the green baize door, and wondered how she could possibly feel such a desire to go to him after he had hoped, so vehemently, that they would never meet again.

There was no time to give it another thought. The kitchen was ordered chaos, with the caterer's men milling around and trays of canapés and tiny sandwiches being filled and filled again.

'It was a delightful party,' observed Lady Wesley to Miss Mudd as she was helped to her bed at two o'clock in the morning—a sentiment not echoed by the hard workers in the kitchen.

A few more days of brilliant sunshine gave way to threatening banks of cloud and an oppressive humidity, with an occasional rumble of far-away thunder. Except for the gardener, who was wishful for a nice drop of rain, the change in the weather wasn't welcome. 'And it'll be more than a nice drop,' declared Cook crossly. 'My corns are shooting something terrible.'

A prophecy fulfilled the following morning with a heavy downpour, which filled the gutters on the roof and turned the gravel sweep before the house into a soggy mess. There was a thunderstorm that night too, and when Molly went over to Sarah's cottage to fetch her a clean apron while she was busy mopping up in one of the attics where there was a leaky tile, she left the door open while she took the apron from a drawer. Charles, rendered jittery by the storm, slid through the doorway and made off.

His absence wasn't discovered for some hours, and it was only then that Molly remembered about leaving the door open. 'He can't have gone far,' she said hopefully. 'Oh, Sarah, I'm that sorry, I'll hunt for him this evening as soon as I've finished my work.'

Sarah said, 'Don't worry, he'll come back. It's going to rain again and he hates getting wet.'

He didn't return that evening and Sarah, wrapped in a borrowed raincoat and with her head tied up in an unbecoming plastic hood, spent the remaining hours of that day searching for him, and at first light was up again scouring the fields and hedges. There was no sign of Charles.

Everyone was very kind—the gardener and the gardener's boy both combed the garden, and even Knott, driving into Bedford on some errand, went slowly, on the look-out for Charles' portly frame. When she had an hour or two off, Sarah went down to the village on Molly's bike, asked if anyone had seen him and left a large notice at the village stores, but there was still no Charles.

He had been missing for three days when Sarah had her day off. She knew exactly what she was going to do. She had early tea with Molly, cut herself some sandwiches, put an apple in her pocket and set off, intent on working her way systematically in a wide circle round the house and the grounds. It was late afternoon and several miles from the house in densely wooded country that she found him, caught in a rabbit snare.

A foot or so from him she stumbled, threw out an arm to save herself and, as she fell, she felt another snare tighten about her arm. She had fallen awkwardly, with the arm flung out behind her in such a fashion that she was unable to get at it, nor could she get any nearer Charles. But, by dint of stretching out the other arm, she was able to slip a finger in the loop around his chest and ease its tightness.

She lay for a minute or two, deciding what to do first. Charles looked in a poor way—if she took her hand away he might struggle, and the wire would tighten and perhaps kill him. On the other hand, without her fingers she wasn't sure how she could free her own arm. She tried gentle tugs, but the wire tightened alarmingly, so she gave that up and lay spreadeagled in the dense hedge, trying to remember if she had passed any farms recently. She had to admit at length that she had been searching a lonely stretch of country for the last half-hour or so, and had seen no living creature, let alone a house.

Stilling a rising panic, she took a good breath and shouted. She shouted at intervals for what seemed like a long time, and the summer day was darkening when she gave up. Charles was silent now, and her finger under the wire had grown numb. 'What a pair of sillies we are,' she told him, speaking in a loud voice to cheer them both up. 'I think we may have to spend the night here. At least there are two of us, and someone must come in the morning.'

The Professor had seen the last of his private patients for the day, and was reading his notes while he drank the cup of tea his nurse had brought for him. When the phone rang he stretched out a reluctant arm, his eyes still on his case-sheets. His 'Nauta' was a thought terse, for he had had a full day and the prospect of a quiet evening and a good dinner might be endangered. But Lady Wesley's voice sounded agitated in his ear, and he said at once, 'Aunt Beatrice—is something wrong? Are you ill?'

'I am worried,' said Lady Wesley. 'Sarah is missing. Her cat, Charles—you know—disappeared three days ago, and although he has been searched for he has still not returned. Sarah had a day off today, and I am told that she left before seven o'clock this morning to look for him—she has not yet returned. I know it's only twelve hours, but she told Molly, the kitchen maid, that she was going to find him at all costs.'

'Has she been searched for?' The Professor's voice was quiet.

'Knott took the car and drove around all the local roads, and two of the local farms he visited said they had spoken to her in the early morning, when she asked them if they had seen the cat. Should I get the police? One hears such awful tales about girls out alone . . .'

The Professor, still very quiet, said, 'No, I'll drive up this evening. I'll leave in half an hour. I'll have Trotter with me—she knows Sarah and she may pick up her scent. The grounds have been searched and the village visited?'

'Of course. Cork organised everything. He is most concerned. Everyone is fond of Sarah—such a sensible girl.'

The Professor gave a bitter little smile and said nothing. 'I'll see you shortly,' he said, and hung up.

He phoned the hospital, spoke to his registrar, left his nurse to close his consulting-rooms and drove himself home, where he told Brindle that he was driving to Lady Wesley's at once and would Mrs Brindle make him a couple of sandwiches and some coffee.

'Shall I pack a bag, sir?' asked Brindle, masking curiosity with a bland face.

'No time. Miss Fletcher and her cat have gone missing. I'm taking Trotter up there—she's pretty good at picking up a scent.'

'An excellent idea, if I may say so. I'll attend to the sandwiches at once, sir.'

Brindle hurried to the kitchen to tell an indignant Mrs Brindle that the delicious meal she had ready for the Professor wasn't going to be eaten, although she brightened at his news. 'Depend on it,' she observed, slicing ham for sandwiches, 'he's taken a fancy to that nice young lady...'

'More than a fancy—I'm of the opinion that he intends to make her his lady wife.'

His wife nodded in pleased agreement.

The Professor, when necessary, could be remarkably quick—he left within the half-hour and, once free of the outskirts of the city, raced up the M1 until he turned off on to the A5140. Shotley Park lay a short distance from the road and only a few miles away. He didn't slacken speed until he drove between the pillars of the front entrance and drew up before the big door.

Cork was waiting for him, his face a mass of worried wrinkles. 'Lady Wesley is in the small sitting-room, sir,' he said, and led the way.

Lady Wesley, who seldom worried about anyone but herself, was uneasy. 'It is so unlike Sarah—she

is a most considerate girl, and would never do anything to inconvenience me.'

The Professor nipped a few sharp words in the
bud and said mildly, 'Well, Aunt Beatrice, I dare
say she has encountered some hindrance and has
been unable to get word to you. I'll take Trotter
and see if I can discover what has happened.'

'But my dear boy, it is past eight o'clock——'

'All the more reason not to waste time. I'll have
a word with Knott if I may, and then be on my
way.' He added gently, 'Don't wait up, my dear,'
and smiled a little at her complacent, 'Indeed I
shan't—this has been a great shock to me.'

The Professor forbore from remarking that it had
been a great shock to him, too.

Knott was in the servants' hall, ringed around
with the rest of them. He produced a map of the
area and offered help. 'We're all that worried, sir,'
he observed. 'Such a nice young lady as Sarah is.
That's right, isn't it, Mr Cork?'

'Indeed, yes. Just say the word, sir, and we'll do
all we can.'

'You have already done a great deal, for we know
where she is not, thanks to your careful searching,
Cork.' The Professor sat down at the table and
studied the map. Presently he said, 'Rabbits—where
do the locals set their snares?'

'Never thought of that,' said Knott. 'On the edge
of Baynard's Wood——' he pointed to the map
'—and here, a bit deeper in and then along the bank
bordering Dingle Farm. A good two miles from
here, that is, and Baynard's Wood is all of four
miles and pretty dense.' His glance fell on Trotter,
sitting patiently by her master.

'Trotter will get through,' said the Professor quietly. 'Now, I shall want a pair of stout gloves, some wire-cutters and some water in a small flask. I have brandy and a torch in the car. And Knott, I shall be glad of your help. I shall go first to Dingle Farm and then on to Baynard's Wood. If I find them I'll bring them back here, but if there is no sign I shall come back here by six o'clock, and we will make further plans. If I find them and there is a telephone within reasonable distance, I shall ring you and ask you to bring my car to the nearest point.'

He took the keys from the pocket and handed them to Knott. 'Cork, you will take any messages, will you not? Phone them through to Dingle Farm if you hear anything before midnight. If it is later than that, I'll leave you to decide what to do for the best. I do not think that Sarah can be very far away, but if we haven't found her by the morning we shall have to alert the police.' He got to his feet. 'I'll be off.'

It was a light evening. He set off at a brisk pace with Trotter, pleased at the idea of a long walk, keeping step. With an eye on the map he began to walk in a wide circle around the grounds of the house, stopping at each small cottage or farm. He was sure that he was on the right track for Trotter, having sniffed at one of Sarah's aprons in the kitchen, had picked up the scent. But although several of the people he asked had seen Sarah very early that morning, no one had seen her since.

The Professor combed the bank bordering Dingle Farm without success, and continued around the perimeter he had marked on the map, pausing every now and then to call and listen, exploring every copse and thicket. It was almost eleven o'clock and a lovely moonlit night when he reached Baynard's Wood. It stretched for a mile or more along the foot of a low hill and extended for twice that distance halfway up it. The Professor patiently walked its length, stopping frequently to call and examine the thick undergrowth, but without success...

At its outermost end he began a slow, difficult process diagonally, going very carefully now, giving Trotter plenty of time. Despite the moonlight, the wood was dark and the undergrowth dense.

They were well into the centre of it, going uphill now, when Trotter checked, gave a rumbling bark and began to push her way into the bushes. The Professor stood still and called, and was rewarded by a faint cry as he set off after Trotter, pushing his way steadily through the bushes. He paused several times to listen, but the dog kept steadily on until she reached a narrow path, almost unused, and trotted ahead, whining.

The Professor, close on Trotter's heels, held Sarah in his torch's beam for a moment, taking in the awkward way in which she was lying and Charles, both of them held by snares. The next moment he was kneeling beside her.

'Keep perfectly still,' he told her, 'while I cut the wire.' He sounded cheerful, ignoring her tear-stained face. 'Any idea how long you've been lying here?'

'It was light,' mumbled Sarah. She gave a hiccuping sob. 'Do please see to Charles.'

He had cut the wire and was running a hand over her arm. 'Nothing broken, I think, but a very nasty bruise. It will hurt for a while, I expect. Now you're going to sit up, ready to hold Charles.'

His matter-of-fact voice acted like a tonic. With his help she struggled up and, with the faithful Trotter blowing softly into her face, watched while the Professor freed Charles, examining him very gently, and then giving him some water and tucking him into her good arm.

'He'll die,' said Sarah in a sad little voice.

'Nonsense. A visit to the vet, several good meals and he will be as good as new. Drink this.'

When she said feebly that she wouldn't, he poured the brandy down her throat. It warmed her even though she coughed and spluttered. 'How did you know I was here?' she asked uncertainly.

'I didn't. Trotter found you.'

'Yes, but how——'

'Don't ask so many questions.' He glanced at his watch. It was very nearly one o'clock in the morning, and there was no hope of getting Sarah and Charles back to any kind of path. With a sigh he sat down beside her and put a great arm around her shoulders. 'As soon as it's light, we'll start for home. Does your arm hurt?'

She nodded, and sniffed forlornly.

'Once the circulation is going again it will feel better.' He uncorked his flask again. 'Drink some more brandy.' And, when she murmured, he insisted, 'Do as I say, Sarah.'

So she drank some more brandy. 'Charles is purring,' she whispered.

'He has every good reason to do so.' The Professor rubbed Trotter's ears, aware that he was perfectly happy, sitting there in a good deal of discomfort with an arm around Sarah and the prospect of a sleepless night before him. He smiled to himself in the darkness—it had been an effort to stay calm when he had found her. He said quietly, 'Close your eyes and go to sleep.'

She tucked her head into his shoulder. 'You won't go away?'

'Don't be silly, girl,' he said very gently.

So she slept with Charles pressed close to her, while the Professor and Trotter sat side by side, waiting for the dawn to break. They were very still, but from time to time the Professor dropped a kiss on to Sarah's tousled head.

CHAPTER NINE

WHEN Sarah woke a pearly dawn was turning to morning, and just for a moment she had no idea where she was. Then she remembered and lifted her face to look at the Professor. He was tired and he needed a shave, but his 'Good morning, Sarah,' was uttered in the cool, polite tones she had heard daily in the clinic at St Cyprian's. It had the effect of making her sit as upright as she could and say in a wooden voice, 'I expect you'd like us to go.' She cast an anxious look at Charles. 'I'm not quite sure where we are . . .'

'I passed a farm about a mile back. Will you stay here while I see if they have a telephone? Knott will bring the car as near as he can, once he knows where we are.' He was taking off his tie as he spoke. 'This will have to do for a sling. Your arm will be painful once you start moving.'

Indeed, it was swollen and bruised, and there was a deep indentation where the wire had bitten into her arm. She had to bite her lip to stop from crying out as he arranged the sling carefully and tied the tie around her neck.

'There's my brave girl.' He kissed her cheek very gently and got to his feet. 'Trotter will stay here to keep you company, and I'll be back as quickly as I can.' He put a hand on the dog's head. 'Stay, Trotter.'

She sat very still after he had gone, afraid to move, her nerves on edge, longing to have a good weep and quite determined not to. Trotter was a comfort, of course, leaning her bulk against Sarah, but she longed for the Professor to come back.

Which he did just as she was at screaming-point.

'Knott is on his way,' he began in a matter-of-fact voice, which prevented the scream just in time. 'There's a lane behind the farm, if you can manage to walk there. It's on the narrow side, but I think he'll manage.' He stooped down and lifted her to her feet. 'There—stand a moment—you must be cramped.'

She stood with his arm around her, feeling odd because her insides were empty, longing for a meal and her bed and a hot bath, and willing to forgo the lot if she could stay just as she was with his arm holding her in a warm, reassuring clasp. After a minute or two she said, 'I'm sure I can walk quite easily.' She looked up at him, and surprised a look on his face which was so quickly gone that she supposed that she must have fancied it.

He said easily, 'All right, let's go,' and began to make his slow, careful way between the trees, his arm still around her shoulders, steadying her.

It seemed to her that they would never reach wherever it was they were going, and after the third stop she asked, 'Is it much further?'

'Ten minutes. Are you all right?'

She nodded—if she said anything now she might burst into a flood of tears. They went on again with Trotter leading the way, and sure enough presently the trees thinned and petered out into a gentle slope covered in bracken and coarse grass, and beyond its further hedge was a rutted lane, little more than a track running past a farm up into the low hills beyond. Knott was there, standing by the Rolls, and he came hurrying forward as soon as he saw them.

'Good man,' said the Professor. 'We'll have to reverse out of here, I suppose?'

'Yes, sir. Sarah's not hurt? And the cat?'

'They're both all right. Let's get her up beside me in front—you get in the back with Trotter. Keep an eye open for me, will you?'

It was a good half-mile before the track opened into a narrow lane, and that in its turn, after a mile or so, joined a wider road. Ten minutes later Sarah was being lifted out of the car and, still with Charles clasped firmly to her, carried through the door of her cottage.

Mrs Legge was already there, waiting for them.

'Bed, after a quick shower,' the Professor said, 'then I'll take a look at that arm. Will you see to that, Mrs Legge?'

'Of course, sir. I'll have Sarah cosy in bed in no time. That's a nasty arm——'

'A rabbit snare.'

Sarah was set down on the bed, and he bent to take Charles. 'I'm going to run this chap to the vet just to make sure that there aren't any bones broken.' At her worried look, he said, 'I'll bring him straight back. Now, be a good girl and do as Mrs Legge tells you.' He smiled at her then with such tenderness that her heart turned over, and then he kissed her cheek and went away.

Mrs Legge, watching, stored this interesting tit-bit away to pass on in the servants' hall presently. If that was the way the wind was blowing, then she for one would be pleased. Romantic thoughts, long buried in Mrs Legge's bosom, took over from her prosaic musing.

Sarah was in her bed, clean and her hair neatly plaited, drinking the tea Parsons had brought over for her and gobbling the bread and butter with it, when the Professor returned. He had Charles with him, tucked under an arm, and he set the cat down on the counterpane.

He nodded at Sarah. 'He's all right. A bit battered, but nothing that won't clear up with food and rest.' He turned to Parsons. 'Do you suppose I might have a cup and share Sarah's tea? And can I leave it to Mrs Legge to let Lady Wesley know that Sarah is back?' He glanced at his watch. 'I must get back to town as soon as possible.'

'I'll find Mrs Legge right away, sir, and bring you some tea and a slice or two of toast, and is there anything else?'

'I'd like to see Knott before I go—perhaps I might come over to the house before I leave.'

'Yes, sir. Do you want Mrs Legge to come over?'

'Er—no, I don't think that's necessary, thank you. I'll let her know if there is anything needed for Sarah.'

Parsons hurried away, bursting to tell everyone that Professor Nauta was going to have his tea with Sarah.

'And why not?' Cork wanted to know. 'After all, he is a professor of medicine and regards Sarah as his patient.'

Parsons buttered the toast. 'If you ask me, he regards her as a great deal more than that.'

'Let us have no gossip,' decreed Mr Cork, at his most severe.

The Professor sat himself on the side of Sarah's bed and took a good look at her. Her face was still pale, and her nose and eyes rather pink. Her hair hung in its plait over one shoulder. He would have liked to have undone the plait and let her abundant hair fall loose, but he reminded himself that this was a professional visit. 'I'll take a look at that arm,' he said with detached civility.

She extended it obediently, wincing because it hurt. 'I'm very sorry,' she said, and was stopped by his,

'Whatever for?'

She went on in a rush, 'You said last time, "Let this be the last time we meet," and I have tried to keep out of your way, really I have.'

He was examining the scratches on her hand where she had tugged at the wire. He asked, without looking up, 'Why?'

She answered him with a touch of peevishness. 'I have just told you...'

He opened his bag and took out impregnated gauze and strapping and covered the weal. 'Not quite all, I think. Ah, here is my tea.'

He gave her instructions while he ate and drank. 'Bed today. You may get up tomorrow, but positively no work. I shall see Mrs Legge before I go, so don't try to do your own thing, Sarah.' He ignored her indignant gasp. 'Charles will be fine by tomorrow; give him small meals every hour or so and let him sleep.'

He got up. 'I must go, I've a round at midday.' He took her hand in his. 'I shall be back, Sarah.'

'I haven't thanked you,' she began.

'Something I look forward to when we next meet.'

'But you don't want to meet——'

'We'll discuss that later. Goodbye, Sarah.'

He had gone and, because she had wanted him to stay and never go away again and her arm ached and she was tired, she had a good cry before she at last went to sleep.

She slept for most of that day, and each time she woke there was someone with an appetising meal on a tray.

During the afternoon Lady Wesley came to see her. 'How fortunate that I decided to telephone Radolf,' she observed complacently. 'I am, when necessary, very quick-thinking, you know, Sarah. He was here very swiftly.' She paused and frowned. 'I very much doubt if he had had time for dinner— so cool and calm too, as though searching for anyone at eight o'clock at night was a perfectly normal thing to do. Of course, Trotter was a great help... Is your arm painful?'

'Only a little, thank you, my lady,' said Sarah in her housemaid's voice. 'I'm sorry to have caused so much trouble.'

Lady Wesley waved a tolerant hand. 'I must say I was most upset when Cork told me that you were missing, but you are a very nice girl, doing work which is not at all suitable for you, and I am most relieved to know that this has ended happily. I understand that Radolf has told Mrs Legge that you are to remain here today, and on no account are you to do any work until he has seen you again.' Her eye fell on the sleeping Charles. 'I am so glad that your cat is safe.'

It seemed to Sarah that no one could do enough for her. A constant stream of visitors came through the door, and whenever anyone had a moment to spare from their duties they popped in. Miss Mudd came with some old copies of *Woman's Own*, Parsons brought some creamed chicken for Charles and Mrs Legge, on an eagle-eyed visit, had a bunch of roses from the gardener.

She put them into a glass jar and studied Sarah as she did so, mindful of the Professor's strict instructions. 'Now, don't you go doing anything silly, Sarah. You stay there in bed, and tomorrow you can get up and dress and sit out in the yard.'

'I could do quite a lot, Mrs Legge,' said Sarah. 'It's only my arm——'

'I'm carrying out the Professor's orders, and him being a very clever doctor, he knows what he's saying, so you'll do as you're told, Sarah.'

Sarah said meekly, 'Yes, Mrs Legge, and please thank Mr Timms for the roses, they're beautiful.'

Mrs Legge nodded briskly. 'And you're to eat every morsel I send over to you. Mr Cork has most kindly decanted a bottle of port for you. You will drink a glass after your supper.'

Sarah said, still meek, 'Yes, Mrs Legge, and please thank Mr Cork for being so kind.'

The port would have come from Lady Wesley's cellar, but all the same it was a kind thought. Sarah drank it and wondered when the Professor would come again. 'Although I must be careful,' she told

Charles. 'I can manage quite well until he smiles at me, but then I go all to pieces.'

Except for her painful arm, she felt quite herself after a good night's sleep and, obedient to Mrs Legge, she got up, dressed with a little help from Parsons and went into the yard with Charles in his basket. It was a lovely day and she would have liked to have gone for a stroll, but Mrs Legge was taking the Professor's instructions seriously. Beyond wandering round the yard, Sarah was forbidden to go further.

That evening she begged Mrs Legge to let her go back to her work in the morning. Mrs Legge was adamant. 'Professor Nauta will give me fresh instructions during the day, Sarah. You may dress, of course, and come over to the house for your breakfast, but you are to do nothing until he gives his permission.'

'Yes, Mrs Legge, but I could shuck the peas for you, and string the beans.'

So she sat in the sun on a patch of grass just beyond the cottages, with Charles stretched out beside her, the bowl of peas on her lap, the pods in a tidy pile in the basket beside her. It was warm in the sun, and if it hadn't been for her heartache over the Professor, she would have been happy thinking about him. When she looked up and saw him standing there, watching her, she didn't quite believe it.

'How funny, I was thinking about you,' she said before she could stop herself. Then rushed on, red in the face, 'What I mean is, I was hoping that you would let me go back to work.'

He smiled then and her heart did its familiar somersault. 'Ah, yes, we have to talk about that. I hear from Mrs Legge that you have been a very good patient.' He came nearer, took the bowl of peas from her and picked up Charles. 'Come with me, Sarah.'

'Why?'

'What a girl you are for asking questions! Come along.'

She got up uncertainly. 'Well, if I must . . . But Mrs Legge is waiting for these peas.'

'Then we'll take them to her.'

So they went through the kitchen door and into the kitchen, where Sarah was surprised to find Cork, Knott, Mrs Legge, Cook, Molly and Parsons—even Miss Mudd was there. They were having their coffee-break early, she supposed. They all smiled at her as she put the peas on the table and she looked uncertainly at the Professor, who said smoothly, 'We shall be back,' and smiled at them all. Then he ushered Sarah out again, and when she opened her mouth to speak said, 'Hush, my dear,' and walked her briskly round to the sweep where the Rolls was parked. 'In you get,' he invited, opening the door for her.

'No,' said Sarah, 'not until I know just what is happening.'

He sighed, shut the door, opened the other door and put Charles on the back seat beside Trotter, then closed that door and faced her.

'We are going home. Somewhere where I should have taken you months ago . . .'

'Home,' breathed Sarah. 'Whose home?'

'Mine—ours, of course.'

'No,' said Sarah quite fiercely, and then, 'Who is Lisse?'

A smile spread over the Professor's handsome features. 'Aha, so that was the sticking-point. Lisse is my sister. She is getting married very shortly, but I think *we* shall marry before then.'

Sarah gaped up at him, then pulled herself together. 'You've started at the wrong end,' she pointed out tartly. 'You haven't even asked me. Besides, you never wanted to see me again.'

He said quietly, 'When I first became aware of you, my darling, I had no wish to marry and yet somehow I found myself thinking of you a great deal, and I didn't want that. I had become set in my ways and I had decided that, unless my dream girl turned up, I would not marry. However, quite soon I had to admit that you were my dream girl, part of my life and then all of it, so that I had no room for doubts.'

'You could have mentioned this,' observed Sarah sharply. 'Especially when you found us in the wood and I—I needed to be comforted.'

'It crossed my mind, my love, but it seemed to me that to get you and Charles back in safe hands was my first care. After all, we shall have the rest of our lives together.' He put his arms around her. 'I love you, darling Sarah. Will you marry me?'

'Yes, oh, yes, I will, Radolf. I love you too.' If she had intended to say more she had no chance, as he bent to kiss her, but presently she lifted her head. 'I shall have to give a week's notice, you know, and there's no one to do my work—it wouldn't be fair——'

'My dearest girl, I gave notice on your behalf when I got here this morning. Aunt Beatrice is sitting at her desk, spreading the news far and wide, and as for the servants' hall, I went to see them before I came to find you. I dare say that even at this moment they are having a whip-round to buy us a butter dish or whatever...'

He looked up as he spoke, and saw Cork withdrawing his head smartly from a window. There was movement behind him, too—they were all there, watching. He bent his head again and kissed Sarah at some length.

'My things,' said Sarah. 'I must pack.'

'Mrs Brindle will have a toothbrush for you. You can buy anything you want tomorrow.' He smiled gently at her. 'I'll get a special licence; we can go down to Minster Lovell and be married there. Now, will you come with me, my dear darling?'

Sarah nodded. Unaware of the delighted faces watching them from the house, she put her arms around his neck and kissed him.

'That was very nice,' said the Professor. 'We must do it again some time.' He opened the car door once again. 'In you get, my darling.'

And Sarah got in.

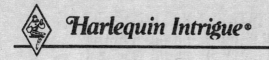

Harlequin Intrigue®

Trust No One...

When you are outwitting a cunning killer, confronting dark secrets or unmasking a devious imposter, it's hard to know whom to trust. Strong arms reach out to embrace you—but are they a safe harbor...or a tiger's den?

When you're on the run, do you dare to fall in love?

For heart-stopping suspense and heart-stirring romance, read Harlequin Intrigue. Two new titles each month.

HARLEQUIN INTRIGUE—where you can expect the unexpected.

This October, Harlequin offers you a second
two-in-one collection of romances

A SPECIAL
SOMETHING

THE FOREVER
INSTINCT

by the award-winning author,

Barbara Delinsky

Now, two of Barbara Delinsky's most loved books are
available together in this special edition that new and
longtime fans will want to add to their bookshelves.

Let Barbara Delinsky double your reading pleasure with
her memorable love stories, A SPECIAL SOMETHING and
THE FOREVER INSTINCT.

Available wherever Harlequin books are sold. TWO-D

HARLEQUIN

Romance

**This October,
travel to England with
Harlequin Romance
FIRST CLASS title #3155
TRAPPED
by Margaret Mayo**

"I'm my own boss now and I intend to stay that way."

Candra Drake loved her life of freedom on her narrow-boat
home and was determined to pursue her career as a company
secretary free from the influence of any domineering man.
Then enigmatic, arrogant Simeon Sterne breezed into her life,
forcing her to move and threatening a complete takeover of her
territory and her heart....